# SAPPHIRE WATER

BOOK FOUR OF THE WITCH BROTHERS SAGA,

ADAM J. RIDLEY

BLAKE ALLWOOD PUBLISHING

Adam J. Ridley
Visit my website at AdamJRidley.com

Printed in the United States of America
Box Elder, SD

First Printing: March 2023

Blake Allwood Publishing

Ebook ISBN:  978-1-956727-40-1
Paperback ISBN:  978-1-956727-41-8
Library of Congress Control Number:  2023901661

Join Blake's email list to get advance notice of new books and receive his occasional newsletter:

www.blakeallwood.com

## MM Romance
## By Blake Allwood

### Transitions Series
Aiden Inspired
Suzie Empowered (MF Romance)
Bobby Transformed

### Chance Series
Love By Chance
Another Chance With Love
Taking A Chance For Love

### Romantic Series
Romantic Renovations (1)
Romantic Rescue (2)
Romantic Recon (3)

### Melody Series
Melody of the Heart
Melody of the Snow

### Road to Rocktoberfest Anthology
Changing His Tune - 2022

### Coming Home Series (2023)
A Long Way Home
Family Home
Discovering Home
Finding Home
Bound For Home
…and many more

### Novellas
Tenacious
Moon's Place

## Romantic Fantasy
## By Adam J. Ridley

### Big Bend Series
Love's Legacy (1)
Love's Heirloom (2)
Love's Bequest (3)

### The Witch Brothers Series
Emerald Earth (1)
Diamond Air (2)
Ruby Fire (3)
Sapphire Water (4)

# ONE

## PROLOGUE: MUIR

### ONE YEAR EARLIER

THE PUPS SAT AROUND the great circle, looking up at the Council of Elders as their leader, Regani, spoke about how important the *coisich mun cuairth*, or walkabout, was to our people. I snickered from my post as head warrior as I watched the enthralled pups react to the stories.

"The Great Fae Queen herself made it a requirement for all Selkie to know our human side as well as our seal," she said.

I remembered being one of those pups and the fear of having to leave the ocean and all I'd ever known. We Selkie were part human, part seal, and part Fae, and would spend almost our entire lives either in or near the sea. Which explained why we were currently in our seal form, listening to the Elders through telepathic imagery rather than actually speaking.

Our seer, Merrow, who'd worn the Dion Adair's stone, had terrifying visions of my walkabout. "You must leave the sea not once but twice," she'd said. At the time, I wasn't much older than the youngsters gathered around the chamber today.

It turned out my *coisich mun cuairth* was quite normal. They sent me to Scotland, where our land guides–humans who knew of the Selkie and helped us–met me. Fascinated, I stayed out of the water three times longer than any other Selkie in our clan's history.

That experience helped me rise quickly through the ranks of warriors. Selkie lived considerably longer than seals or humans. Our average life span was around a century and a half. As such, our people usually reached a mature age before ascending to positions of leadership.

The old Selkie I replaced hadn't taken the head warrior position until he was in his fortieth year. I was only twenty. I owed most of that to Merrow, who, before she passed, told the Council of Elders that the survival of the Selkie depended on it.

The pups' laughter pulled me out of my thoughts. Laughter at Regani's stories was good, considering the *coisich mun cuairth* was a serious and often scary subject.

Regani motioned for one of the other leaders to begin telling the pups our clan's history. Unlike humans, who didn't seem to respect or understand the importance of learning about the past, the Selkie considered knowing our interwoven histories imperative to our survival.

Selkie had lived alongside humans for most of our existence. Now, the humans had forgotten the old ways and seemed determined to destroy everything around them. At least, that was what the Elders taught us, and that was what I'd seen during my limited time on land.

I sighed and turned my attention back to the Elder who was telling the children how the Dion Adair, a half-Selkie, half-witch, had escaped his parents' fate by taking his deceased father's pelt as his own.

His Selkie father and witch mother had lived at a time in human history when Christians had persecuted witches. Neither had been able to save themselves from the witch hunters. Legend had it that his mother had given her lover back his pelt just before her capture to be burned at the stake. Instead of abandoning her, however, he cast his pelt aside and burned with her.

According to the legend, that act had done two things. For the Dion Adair, then just a boy, it solidified a bone-deep hatred for the humans who occupied the land. And, because his father had willingly shucked his pelt, the boy was able to use it to become a Selkie. At least, in part, and the Selkie embraced him as one of their own.

His human practicality, combined with the magic inherited from his mother, worked to benefit our people. He helped the Selkie organize and control their movements to ensure stronger, more dependable protections. To this day, the Dion Adair's power still protected the sleeping grounds. Or at least, it had until recently.

He had predicted a day would come when his unique combination of magical forces would fail. The Selkie had their own magic, of course, but it was never meant to create or maintain barriers. Our magic was more associated with the sea and fending off predators like sharks, helping life flow, and keeping a balance in the ocean. Those limitations, however, now threatened our very existence.

The story of the Dion Adair had always disturbed me. A Selkie's pelt was his own, our skin when in seal form, and I couldn't imagine another creature wearing my seal skin.

As a child, I'd questioned why the father's pelt didn't die with him, and the same Elder had explained usually, that was exactly what would happen. Upon death, one's pelt would die too. Somehow though, probably because the young Dion Adair had slipped the pelt on at the moment of his father's death, it had accepted him.

Now, that same pelt lay in a deep cavern, far below the water's surface, where it waited for the second Dion Adair. Though the first Dion Adair had no offspring, he had siblings who'd escaped the witch hunts and gone on to live among humans. An ancient seer had foretold of a descendant of one of these siblings, who carried the bloodline of the first Dion Adair's father, would one day claim the pelt as his own. When that day came, this new Dion Adair would save the Selkie from annihilation.

Of course, it was easy just to let the legends remain in the past, recounted through the generations as awe-inspiring or fearsome tales, but nothing more. I had no idea what the future held, but because Merrow had linked my destiny with that pelt, I knew I should pay close attention as the Elders told and retold the old stories.

# Two

— · —

## Present Day: David

DAYS WERE DARK AFTER my mom had died. I was finishing my master's degree in marine biology at the time. My stepfather wanted me to go into medicine as he, Mom, and his kids had. Mom had too, but at least she'd come to accept it and told him to back off the criticizing once I'd been accepted into the program.

Of course, after she was gone, all bets were off. Mom had come from money, but she hadn't signed a prenup or had a will. She'd created a trust for me when I was born that had grown to a significant amount, but it was designated for college expenses only.

The animosity between my stepfather and me had become nearly unbearable, and I'd be damned if I wasn't going to spend every last cent in that trust fund. So, instead of entering the job market and pursuing the career I wanted, I found a Ph.D. program in Oregon, was accepted, and left, never to look back.

Fortunately, I'd gotten a job right out of grad school, taking tourists on tours of the resident gray whale pod. It didn't pay a lot, but with some careful saving between that and my marine biology research work, it was enough to buy a home precariously perched atop extinct volcanic cliffs along the coast.

I got it for a song, probably because the cliff would eventually erode enough that my home would plunge into the ocean. Or, more accurately, the lagoon between my cottage and the beach. For now, though, I was content enough simply being a homeowner.

"David, sweetheart, are you here?" I recognized Marta's voice instantly and smiled.

"I'm around back."

With her bright red hair, she bounced around the corner of my cottage. "Oh good, I was afraid you weren't here."

"What can I do for you?" I asked as she approached me, leaning over for a cheek kiss.

"Ugh, you're all sweaty."

"Marta, it's over a hundred degrees. Of course, I'm sweaty."

"Don't get haughty. I knew you'd be doing something stupid like working out in the sun. That's why I took the day off to check on you."

"Fuss at me, more like," I said and felt a little buzz, which was Marta's way of telling me she was powerful enough to zap me hard if I pushed too far, something I did every chance I got.

"You need to be more careful with that," I said, waving my hands toward her as my way of describing her magical abilities.

She just shook her head and rolled her eyes as usual. "I'm going in to fix us a drink. I suggest you come in before you get heat stroke or something."

I couldn't help but smile. In this part of the world, everything stopped if it hit eighty degrees. Where I'd grown up, it regularly topped over a hundred with the bonus of humidity you could practically cut with a knife. A hundred degrees here meant I could get a nice tan while doing some maintenance on the cottage. I'd be doing nothing else now that Marta was here, though.

After cleaning up, I sat across from my best friend and smiled at seeing the sandwich she'd made me. "Sometimes you act like my mom or something," I argued, knowing I'd get the eye roll again.

"Just because I worry when you're being a total twit doesn't mean I'm... you know what? Forget it. I'm not doing that argument again. Instead, I wanted to tell you about a dream I had."

This time I rolled my eyes. Marta was a powerful witch who'd taught me some things over the years. Although I argued that I didn't have much skill, I was surprised to find I'd been pretty good at chanting and casting spells. I firmly believed in Marta's gifts, but still liked messing with her.

"Okay, tell me your mumbo-jumbo dream." The hairs on my neck stood up as a wave of electricity flitted through me. "Hey, what was that for?" I asked, rubbing my neck.

"To remind you I'm a powerful witch, and you shouldn't make light of my abilities, or in this case, my premonitions."

I chuckled. "Okay, in all seriousness, what's the dream?"

She gave me a stern look, as if she was debating telling me, then sighed. "I dreamed a dark mist drifted around your home, which I could tell was meant to represent you. There were dark shapes in the mist, things that wanted to hurt you, kill you even." She hesitated a moment, as if unsure about telling me more. "It's darker than what normally floats around you." She took a sip of her iced tea and, ignoring my scowl, continued, "David, this is serious. Something's coming that wants to hurt you. It's not like a bad person or people, it's something wielding magic. I wish you'd stop being stubborn and come to Chemeketa with me so someone more experienced with divination can take a look."

I put my hand up. "Marta, I'm a scientist. Yes, I concede you've convinced me I have some talents I hadn't anticipated, but Chemeketa is too close to where I work. I can't be hanging out with your hippie friends, chanting over fires, or dancing naked under the moon. If the wrong people were to see that..."

"Stop. First, I've told you a thousand times, Chemeketa is secretive with its gifts and for good reason. No one outside the magical community knows. You'd be safe."

"You can't guarantee that, and I can't risk losing my job. I'm sorry, Marta, I'm not willing to go to Chemeketa, and if something wicked this way comes, I'll deal with it when it gets here. For real, what would anything magical care about me anyway? I'm barely able to use the spells you've taught me."

We both knew I was downplaying my gifts, but it was not like Marta could stand guard over me twenty-four seven anyway. She opened her mouth to argue, then shut it again before getting up to put her plate and glass next to the sink. "Listen to what I tell you," she said when she returned to the table. "You are a newbie, and therefore you've never had to face the dark side of magic. I understand your hesitation and respect your lack of desire to be involved, but my dream was a warning I want you to take seriously. Promise me you'll think about it." I nodded, and she squeezed my shoulder. "I'll come back in a couple of days after I've had time to prepare things to help keep you as safe as I can here. You'll at least let me put up protective shields, right?"

I shrugged, which she took as a yes. Ultimately, I thought she knew I wouldn't fight her too hard. The only exception was letting Marta's magical community know about my latent talents. I wasn't quite ready for that, and doubted I ever would be.

# THREE

— · —

## MUIR


"YOU'RE GOING TO HAVE to find the Dion Adair."

"What?" I asked, staring dumbfoundedly at Regani, our minds connected.

"You heard me fine, Muir. Our new seer has dreamed it, so we can no longer wait. The boundaries have already begun to fall, and if they collapse entirely, none of us will be safe."

"But, how?" I asked. "Did the young seer ascertain who he is, where he is? How will I know when I find him?"

Regani didn't answer me right away, she just continued making her way up the beach of the familiar secluded cove our people had accessed for generations. Without warning, she removed her pelt, and I gasped in shock. In all my time on the security force, I'd never seen a councilmember remove their pelt in front of me. Normally it was done in private, because, even within our community, fear of losing one's pelt prevented anyone from taking the chance of becoming that vulnerable. Not knowing the proper protocol for such an unprecedented move, I quickly followed suit by removing my pelt as well.

Regani and I were now naked in our human form, as all Selkie were upon shifting, but for a chain that hung around her neck. The Dion Adair's stone, a sparkling blue sapphire, dangled from it. "Wear this. It will guide you to the Dion Adair," she said, unclasping the chain, "But know this, it won't protect you from your enemies. You must travel quickly and stay out of sight. Am I clear?"

I nodded, fear gripping me, but also excitement. I already knew from Merrow's prophecy that I'd one day be given a quest, and that time had finally come.

"I will do my best," I said as Regani draped the chain and stone around my neck. She promised to inform my warriors of my immediate and hopefully temporary absence, but said I should inform my family directly.

After we returned to our seal form, I rushed home to say my goodbyes to my parents and siblings. If this solo expedition turned out to be as perilous as anticipated, there was a decent chance I wouldn't make it back alive. We'd all understood since I was a pup that this was my destiny, but I still wanted to ensure my family knew how much I loved and would miss them should the worst happen.

Back at the cove, I hauled out onto the shore and shifted from my seal form before slipping silently through the new moon darkness until I reached the great standing stones. I lay prostrate under the stones, my human body naked, and waited for any visions that might help me on my quest.

I must've fallen asleep, because I knew I was dreaming. A man's hands slid over my chest before moving to my back and pulling me into an embrace. It was an intimate touch, and considering I'd never mated with a human, even when I was on my *coisich mun cuairth*, I was surprised by how good it felt. How right.

I woke with a start and wiped at the sweat that drenched my body. "Well, that's interesting," I said out loud, quickly looking around to make sure no humans had heard me. Luckily, while the standing stones had become a daytime tourist attraction, they were usually deserted at night.

I snuck unseen back to the inlet, found my pelt I'd stashed safely behind a boulder just below the surface of the water, and slipped it back on. I had no idea why the ancestors had chosen to show me an intimate encounter, but I'd take it over an ominous vision. Maybe it was the Dion Adair I was making love to, maybe it was just to fortify me for the long journey ahead, or maybe it was a sign of things to come.

# Four

## David

THE FOG CRAWLED ACROSS the great monoliths, and up the ancient volcanic slopes to the cliffs and the trees where my cottage sat. Despite the current heatwave, which had initially pushed the fog out to sea, the cooling mist had returned today for at least the early morning hours.

Fog has always attracted me. In my childhood hometown it was rare, but when it did roll through, I hungered to be in the thick of it. Once when I was three, according to my mom, I disappeared in the wee hours of the morning. It was early fall and the warm earth had been hit by a cold front during the night.

They searched and called for me throughout the morning, but didn't find me until the sun finally burned the fog off. I was lying against the back of a large oak tree, fast asleep.

My great-grandmother on my mom's side was Irish. I had only scattered memories of her since she died when I was still a young child, but I did remember her telling me my body missed the homeland. "One day, you'll need to return," she said as she cradled my cheek in her wrinkled hand.

I visited Ireland when I was a teen and loved it, of course, but the island hadn't called to me.

I knew my destiny wasn't in my home state of Tennessee but, unfortunately, it wasn't in Ireland either, despite my heritage. I felt more at home in Oregon than anywhere else. I was still a bit of a duck out of water, but at least my innate love of the sea, mixed with my affinity for the coastal weather, made me feel less so.

Pacific Northwest fog was unique, different from Tennessee and the old country as well. It felt newer, more anxious, and almost playful as it came rolling in off the powerful Pacific Ocean. As though change came quickly here and, like the land, everything was continually evolving.

Life in and around the ocean perfectly represented the circle of life. For someone like me, who'd spent my life researching how the creatures of the sea interacted, the natural forces at play were nothing less than terrifying and fascinating. Each had its place and served a purpose, most as both predator and prey, but for the select few at the top of the food chain, and even then, pollution, overfishing, and manmade disasters always threatened to upset the balance.

While the fog made me feel more at home here, I definitely didn't think my great-grandmother was right. It never made me think of our ancestral homeland. I did think it helped me hide from the darkness that'd plagued me all my life, though. I chalked most of that up to never knowing my birth father well. He'd abandoned me and Mom when I was about five. I only knew him through fragmented memories, a few photographs, and a handful of details from Mom, so it was no surprise she had given me her maiden name as my surname.

My great-grandmother had seen the darkness in me and called it such, although looking back at it, I just assumed that was her old-fashioned way of referring to depression. But I wasn't depressed, I just felt... off. That was the only way I knew how to describe it.

Only amid the swirling sea fog did I feel completely at ease. There, I felt whole.

Unfortunately, today, the fog didn't carry its usual smoothing qualities. Instead, it was haunting. I could hear, no, it was more like I could actually *feel* the sounds of pain and suffering in the cool mist. I shook my head at my fanciful thoughts. Marta's dreams were clearly beginning to get to me.

I grabbed my pack and walked down my self-made trail to the tiny beach that skirted my property, and hesitated with a realization that as the fog thickened, so did my sense that there really was something sinister about it. If I were to put an emotion to it, I'd say the fog felt... angry.

Fear gripped me as I walked through the maliciousness that hung in the air. I'd always had the gift of discernment, or so my great-grandmother had surmised when I'd told her I thought a place was scary. I could sense where dark and light energy existed, even millennia after it had passed, and feel when entities were present.

My great-grandmother had accepted my abilities without question, so I figured this link to the paranormal, or "hokey pokey" as I thought of it, must've come from her side of the family. That unexplainable element in my own life was why I didn't bat an eye when, after becoming good friends with Marta, she'd admitted to being a witch and said she recognized some of those same qualities in me. In time, she began teaching me how to harness and wield my gifts, though I was still far from skilled. She'd also disclosed details about Chemeketa, a safe haven community for witches and elementals, though I still felt reluctant to visit there.

As I walked closer to the shore, I could feel the darkness giving way to the pain that had called to me from above. I felt it radiating from the sea cave that was submerged during high tide. The inside of the cave sloped upwards, which I found out once when I'd been stuck in it as the tide changed. I was able to stay out of the water that time, but I figured even the more elevated levels that sheltered me would be underwater during the highest tides.

I wandered down to the mouth of the cave and cautiously peered inside. The tide would be low for another hour, so I set my watch alarm for thirty minutes to warn me. I needed to be out of the cave before then, or I'd either be spending the night perched on a rock ledge or swimming against the current.

I fished a flashlight out of my pack, then slowly climbed into the cave and looked around. There was... was that a trail of blood? Uneasiness churned in my gut, but I pressed on. The trek in was steep, climbing almost fifteen feet within moments of entering. I wondered how or why a creature from the sea would climb inside even if they were injured. I decided caution should be my first approach, so turning my flashlight off, I turned on the red light I kept in my pack. Most creatures couldn't see the red light, and I was hoping I didn't startle whatever I might find into attacking me.

As it turned out, it was me who startled when I saw a man lying on his side, naked and bleeding. I ignored my gut reaction to run away and instead moved toward him. When I got a better look at his wounds, I could also sense internal injuries and the darkness pulsating from them. At that point, I knew he was dying.

Other than a very basic first aid kit, though, I had no medical tools to help him. I doubted I could get the man out of the cave in time for emergency services to arrive, not that they could treat magic-induced trauma anyway. With no other choice, I would have to rely on my... other abilities.

I usually ignored my skills, preferring to allow nature to proceed as it should rather than interfere with the natural order. But this was an injured human being, or human-like being, at least, and my hand was forced. That I sensed his injuries were caused by something unnatural only furthered my resolve to intervene.

The man didn't stir as I knelt beside him and placed my hands on his torso, allowing the power to flow through me, out of my heart and into my hands. When he didn't respond, I allowed my consciousness to connect with his.

"I'm here to help. I'm going to try to heal you," I said in the language of dreams.

The man was guarded but I felt his acknowledgment even though he prevented me from seeing or feeling anything else about him.

I concentrated my efforts on his wounds. I wasn't strong magically, at least not strong enough to heal him completely, nor had I practiced using my gift for this level of care. But I'd do the best I could for this man, because I was all he had.

I focused first on removing the darkness from the wounds. I attacked the dark with light that came from within me in a blinding burst, momentarily lighting the cave like a grenade. When the light subsided, the darkness had been extracted, and its oily, sick scent of death was replaced with the smell of ozone.

The darkness had been a poison, and some tissue had already been infected. I pushed light into the dying tissue until I could feel it was clean. Then I began the rough process of mending the man's wounds. I started internally, ensuring all his organs and severed arteries were healed to prevent internal bleeding. The effort pulled on my resources, zapping me of energy, and I cursed internally for not actively practicing my abilities.

I had to rest for a moment, and just as I bowed my head, my alarm went off. I turned it off, prayed the incoming tide wouldn't climb the fifteen feet to reach us, then resigned myself to being temporarily stuck in the cave again.

I grounded my spirit, allowing myself to connect to the fire and water elements that were still strong in this part of Oregon where volcanic lava had once touched the sea, and chastised myself for not thinking of that earlier. Forgetting to ground myself before practicing my gift was a constant for me. Family legend had it that my great-grandmother had been a wise woman, but she hadn't been around long enough to give me any instruction. So, I'd only really had Marta's mentorship, but even that had been limited.

I'd met Marta by chance at her shop in Florence, not long after I'd moved to the Oregon coast. In the years since, she'd shown me how to ground, pulling energy from the earth or the sea instead of using my own. I still tended to forget, however, and as a result, like now, I exhausted myself before finishing what I was doing.

I could hear the tide returning to the lower reaches of the cave and had to push the fear from my consciousness, refocusing on grounding and absorbing the energies from the two elements. I sat back on my heels, closing my eyes, shifted my absorption to water, the element that seemed to resonate with me the most, and allowed the water's energy to fill me.

As always, I lost track of time, but when I opened my eyes, I was strong enough to help the man again.

I focused on his injuries and allowed the grounded connection with the sea to flow into him. Though he looked like a human man, the sense of power emanating from the ocean confirmed I must be working on a creature of the sea.

I felt his consciousness react to the healing as I stitched up the nasty gashes that tore his flesh. No matter how fast or slow, there was a process to healing. My mom, stepfather, and stepsiblings, all of whom worked in medicine, had talked about it at the dinner table, so I knew speeding up the process caused intense pain. Unfortunately, because I was too inexperienced to remember to ground before I reacted, the healing process had taken longer than it should've.

Once I finished mending the wounds as much as possible, I sensed before I saw the pelt lying on the floor near where it sloped toward the bottom of the cave.

"You're a Selkie. Why would you be in these waters?" I asked him aloud, but got no answer.

I didn't know much about the Selkie, other than they existed, plus some random tidbits Marta had imparted, but I did know their pelts were practically sacred. Something to handle with care and respect. I gently picked up the pelt, observing the same pattern of lacerations that had sliced the man's skin, then laid it out and allowed the sea's energy to flow into it through me. It shocked me that healing the pelt took more energy than healing the man.

When the pelt was as healed as I could get it, a wave of fatigue hit me, almost causing me to topple over. Exhausted mentally and physically, I sat next to the man, who still showed no signs of consciousness.

"We're stuck here together, seal man," I said, more to myself than him.

The chill in the cave was intense. Using magic sometimes drained me of warmth, depending on how much of myself I had to put into it. When I touched the man lying prostrate next to me, he felt cold. I had no idea if Selkie suffered from hypothermia, but I sure could.

I cursed myself again for not being better prepared. I only kept a small blanket in my pack, not big enough to cover us both lying side by side. The ranger safety courses I took as an intern in Washington State's Olympic National Park taught me that when someone was hypothermic and you couldn't get help, you stripped them and used your own body heat to warm them up.

I ensured the pelt was nearby, assuming he'd wake before me and want to return to the sea as quickly as possible. Hopefully it could continue the healing process where my skills had failed.

I stripped, laying my clothing underneath me before pulling the man into my embrace and wrapping my legs around his. I then tugged the blanket over the top of us, creating what I hoped would be enough of a warm cocoon to survive the night. Thankful that Marta had forced me to learn the basics, I had enough energy and power left to add another layer of warmth to us. I pulled from the ocean's energy and felt the warmth around us increase although only slightly. *Maybe*, I thought to myself, *I need to pay more attention to this magic thing after all.*

As I fell asleep, with every inch of me pressed against the Selkie, I became keenly aware of the muscular body I held tightly in my arms. He smelled of something rich and almost musty mixed with the scent of the sea, and I couldn't help but inhale deeply. If I hadn't been so exhausted, I knew I'd have felt the zing of sexual attraction.

My last thought was that I should've hidden his pelt until I had a chance to see him better, perhaps even speak to him once morning came, but it wasn't meant to be. What little strength I had left was moving me toward sleep and rejuvenation.

# FIVE

## MUIR

I FELT THE FIRM press of a warm human body flush against mine and woke with a start in the arms of a man. As much as I relished the feeling of his embrace, fear also gripped me.

"When a Selkie's pelt is stolen, he can't return to the sea until he finds it again." The words of my grandfather echoed in my ears.

There was too much at stake for me to risk losing my pelt. As I pulled away from the man, I felt the energy surrounding us and knew he was no ordinary human. He was a witch and an incredibly handsome one at that.

I'd long been attracted to human men, but our kind didn't tend to mix with theirs. Well, not unless they lost their pelts and fell in love with their captors. The Elders often recounted such legends, but more in warning than as romantic tales. No known incidents had happened in centuries, though, and for good reason.

The spread of Christianity in the Emerald Isle had caused the island's people not to see Selkie in the same way as during Pagan times. Over time, but for a few prac- titioners of the old ways, whose descendants would become our modern-day land guides, most humans came to view us with fear, uncertainty, or questioned our existence. Our people had also become much more ruthless with societal rules. We were given specific areas to live and rest. No longer were we allowed to sleep in any sea cave we found. Ironically, it was a half-blood—the Dion Adair—who'd initiated the rules in order to ensure our safety.

But as Regani had told the pups, even though we Selkie were creatures of the sea, we must also come ashore from time to time. Taking human form and reconnecting with our human past was equally important to maintaining our overall health.

I stared at the handsome man who still lay asleep beside me and shook my head. Humans weren't our real enemy. At least, they weren't knowingly trying to obliterate us. That title went to an older, more evil foe. We call them *Dorcha* in Gaelic, the dark ones. Throughout our existence, Dorcha and Selkie had been bitter enemies, and many wars were fought between our peoples over the centuries. We won the last few and pushed the dark ones out of the North Atlantic.

While we shared much in common, the Dorcha had certain advantages over us. They didn't have to leave the sea to rest on land, and more importantly, they could shift themselves into any sea creature. We had always only been seals. They were not immune to the ways of man any more than we were, though.

The Dorcha had regularly taken the form of whales as a disguise to largely avoid natural predators, which for a time put them at considerable risk. Many were killed during the human Victorian era, when whaling ships swept through the North Atlantic seeking whales for their blubber, though the Dorcha fought back. One story I heard while on my *coisich mun cuairth* told of a mad white whale who fought a brave human captain. It was obviously embellished and was mostly the stuff of fantasy, but there was an underlying truth to it as well.

I reached up to where the chain had once hung around my neck, and the same surge of grief and loss I'd felt when it'd been pulled off of me during the attack swept through me again. The Dion Adair's stone was gone. It'd been painful to wear when in seal form, but the moment it clasped to my body, embedding itself underneath my pelt, it had shown me visions. I'd swam wherever it led until I reached these shores.

During my journey, shark and orca frequently swam close to check me out. Both hungered for the seal I appeared to be, but were baffled when my Selkie powers reached out and tamed them. This part of the world had never, to my knowledge anyway, encountered a Selkie. It was no wonder the sea life here was so confused by me.

The abundance of salmon in these waters was a welcome change from back home. I could only imagine how excited my family would be to hunt salmon so easily.

Dorcha found me one night as I swam after the fish I planned to feast on for my evening meal. I was completely unaware of the Dorcha's presence, distracted by the hunt and having lived so many years without fear of them.

Because I was unprepared, the Dorcha in the form of a great white shark sliced me to pieces before I could defend myself. The towering sea stacks lining the coast saved me as I darted behind one, drawing up what energy I could. When the Dorcha attacked, I lashed out, pushing the dark one back into the rocky sea stack.

Not knowing how long I'd be able to fend off the larger, vicious creature, I began swimming for my life. That was when a pod of orca came to my rescue. They circled their prey before making their attack, dragging the dark one deep into the abyss.

Pain seared through me as I continued swimming toward the shore and into the cave as the tide began to go out. I crawled up a steep incline until I felt I was above the tide, knowing, in my human form, I could drown just like any other human.

I had just enough energy to pull my pelt off and only then realized that the Dion Adair's stone was missing. Through anguished tears, more from the loss of the stone than my own imminent death, I thrust my powers out to find my connection with the sea. Before I could do anything about the stone, I fell unconscious.

Sometime after I'd collapsed, even though I was neither awake nor asleep, I felt a fresh wave of pain rip through me. Someone was reaching out to me, and I immediately connected with his male energy. Pain lanced through me anew, but this time, I could sense it came from cleansing and healing.

As I lay awake now, though considerably sore, I could tell I'd been healed enough to move. Seeing my pelt, I extracted myself from the man's arms, then grabbed it and rushed as quickly as I could toward the ocean I could hear just steps away. It was high tide and luckily, he hadn't hidden my pelt before... before saving me.

This man, a human man, had *clearly* saved my life. He must be a powerful witch to do such a thing. I looked at my pelt, sure I'd see gashes in it, but, apparently, he'd healed that too. I was confused as to why he would do that. It also meant the witch knew my true nature, yet had taken no measures to trap me. How strange. His actions didn't match anything I'd learned about humans. Even on my *coisich mun cuairth*, I found humans to be selfish by nature.

No matter how selfless he'd been last night, I couldn't take a chance that he'd wake up and attempt to trap me now. My quest was too important for that. And yet, I couldn't deny the pull I felt toward this man. Something primal.

*Bugger it*, I thought to myself, remembering the slang I'd learned while on my walkabout. I looked back at the man, who peacefully slept where I'd left him, and once again, I noticed how beautiful he was—slight, with muscles that rippled gently over his naked flesh.

I'd had both male and female lovers, as such preferences were never a concern among Selkie. In human form, I preferred the look and feel of men. However, during my *coisich mun cuairth* in the Scottish isles, their customs seemed to discourage such mating, which meant while on land I'd remained celibate.

Gazing upon the man who had used his body to keep me warm all night, I felt a deep attraction. I'd hungered for companionship since leaving my family and spending long months out to sea, and seeing this man only intensified that loneliness.

After storing my pelt where it was too dark for human eyes to see, I laid my body across from him, watching him sleep until I dozed myself. Finally, he stirred, waking me, and I opened my eyes to see the deepest blue pools I'd ever seen staring back at me. Selkie, much like seals, had dark brown eyes. Gazing into his blue orbs startled and enchanted me.

"You're better then?" he asked in English.

I nodded.

"Good," he said as he sat up and stretched, moaning as the blood drained from his face. "That might have been too much magic for me," he added as he carefully eased himself back down, looking at the cave ceiling.

I crawled over and laid my hand on his chest, allowing the sea's energy to flow through me into him.

He sighed in pleasure, his beautiful eyes never leaving mine. When I finally broke the gaze to check on his recovery, my eyes rested on his erect cock. My energy causing his arousal had the same effect on me, and when I met his eyes again, they'd become dark with lust.

Leaning over, I took the man's mouth with mine as my hand slid down his body, intent on giving him pleasure.

My mouth followed my fingers, kissing down his strong chest and across his taut abs before reaching my true destination. He moaned with pleasure as I took his length deep into my throat, swallowing as though I'd just caught a fish in my seal form.

He allowed me to continue for several minutes before pulling me up, and rolling his body on top of me. He ground his cock into mine, his mesmerizing eyes never leaving mine.

"You are so handsome," he said before he slipped down my body, and impaled his mouth on my cock just as I'd done to him. Eventually, he allowed me to wiggle out from under him and flip around, taking his cock in my mouth at the same time as he had mine.

We pleasured each other until we both came, simultaneously, which was always a bonus. I slurped his come down, swallowing it with pride. When I leaned up, I noticed he seemed to have done the same.

Our coupling was fast, as was common with Selkie. During my *coisich mun cuairth*, I noticed humans seemed to equate more meaning to acts of intimacy than we did, but this man had let me take charge. He also didn't appear to regret what we'd done.

We both dozed in and out of sleep until I heard the tide flowing out, and decided I could no longer delay taking my leave.

"Wait," the man said. "What's your name?"

Despite having saved me and our shared intimacy only moments ago, I was still wary of this male witch. He had great power. Power that could certainly do some significant damage to me if I were to overstay my welcome.

"I'm Muir Fen, Selkie of the Scottish isles. What is your name, human?" I asked.

The man smiled. "You're from Scotland. I should've known you weren't from around here. I'm David, and my people are originally from Ireland."

His heritage alerted me to his potential significance, especially since he was a witch. Since I'd lost the Dion Adair's stone, I couldn't look into the blue sapphire to see if this man was the one I'd been sent to find. But I cautiously allowed myself to hope maybe divine providence had led me to him for that reason.

"What part of Ireland do your people hail from?" I asked.

"From many parts, I think. My great-grandmother, she's the one who told me the most about our Irish roots, was born on Tory Island. You probably know it as Toraigh."

I drew in a deep breath, causing him to look at me strangely. Toraigh was the island where they burned the witch and her Selkie husband, the Dion Adair's parents.

When I didn't respond further, the man–*David*–stood to get dressed. "I need to get going. I'm afraid the tide will return soon, and I'd rather not spend another night trapped in this cave. Not all of us have seal skins to slip into."

He winked, and I knew he was teasing me. Selkie weren't what you'd call humorous people, but my time on land had shown me that land-locked humans tended to make light of awkward situations.

"Why didn't you hide my pelt?" I asked, curious as to why he was allowing me to leave, especially after he'd exerted so much energy to save me.

David shrugged before slipping on his thin coat. "I don't need a seal person being pissed at me for keeping him away from his home. Besides, as a gay man, I like my hookups to leave when we're done, going on their way come morning."

I didn't know the word hookup, but I assumed it related to mating practices. Was he calling me a whore?

"I'm not one to lie with just anyone, if you're thinking that."

My people weren't as caught up in the concept of monogamy as humans, but when we found and committed ourselves to a loved one, we didn't stray. I wondered why this man thought he should insult me, though.

He smiled and his cheeks reddened. "I wasn't saying that. My apologies if I sounded rude. I was talking more of myself. I like being alone."

"Oh, I see. I, too, prefer to be alone. When I am not with my family."

David nodded and turned to go.

"Wait," I said, concerned I might lose the man I'd come so far to find. "I must ask for your assistance one last time. I have been hunted by one of the dark ones, and require more rest before I can safely return to the sea. Do you have a place where I could recuperate?"

I was stretching the truth. The Dorcha who'd attacked me was no longer a threat, the orca pod had ensured that, though I suspected more were likely lurking close by. And if this witch knew much about my people, he'd know I'd be more comfortable recuperating in the cave than in a human dwelling, away from the ocean. But I trusted him, he'd proven himself to be a friend, and if he was the man I sought, I couldn't pass up the chance to get to know him.

When he stared at me for several long moments, I thought maybe he'd say no. Instead, he looked toward the opening of the cave and sighed. "I know you're telling the truth. I can still feel the... is it anger? I'm warning you, though, I also don't want you stuck here once you're better, so keep your pelt close. If you leave it here, some tourist is likely to find it and make off with it."

The man clearly didn't know the Selkie. We were never that careless with our pelts. Our lives as creatures of the sea depended on it.

Without another word, David thrust his pack toward me, and I bundled my pelt into it. After he told me to wrap myself in the blanket from the night before, I then followed him through the cave entrance and up the beach toward his dwelling.

# Six

— . —

## David

I QUIETLY KICKED MYSELF for interfering. Yes, the quickie was damn good, and yes, I felt good about helping this, well, *Muir*, but I didn't want a roommate. Every story I'd read about the Selkie told of them leaving when they found their pelts, not moving in with you. I shook my head. So much for stupid legends.

I led the way up the cliff to my cottage, resisting the urge to look back at the attractive figure walking mostly naked behind me.

When we finally got home, I led Muir directly to the guest bedroom. "You can sleep here," I said, then turned to leave him on his own.

"Where will you be sleeping?" he asked.

"In my bed."

"I thought I might be sharing your bed after this morning." I could see the confusion on the Selkie's face.

*Of course*, I thought to myself. "Listen, I admit I don't know much about the Selkie, and the legends I've heard are obviously way off. I'm not sure what you expect but I'm a modern man, a man of science. I don't want to be a part of all this magic mumbo jumbo."

Muir's confused expression only deepened. "But you're a witch, and a very powerful one."

"A witch... of all things," I muttered in disbelief. I wasn't exactly sure what I was, but my abilities were child's play next to Marta's, and she was the only witch I knew.

"You refuse to acknowledge the gifts you possess, and yet I would not have survived without your intervention. Thank you for saving my life," he said, sounding so sincere that I nearly caved in my resolve to keep him at arm's length.

"Okay, let's do this," I said in an effort to set some boundaries. "Why don't you store your pelt in the guest room? You can come and go as you see fit, and I'll even help you find a place to hide it in the rare event anyone visits. Meanwhile, I'll get you some clothes to wear while you're in human form."

Muir nodded, and I left him in the guest room to find some sweatpants and a t-shirt he could wear. Not that I minded looking at his incredibly fit body, but I needed to keep my head on straight when I set out the boundaries for us living together.

After he'd dressed and came to sit across from me at the kitchen table, I asked, "Do you know how to live in a modern dwelling? I mean, do you know how to use a toilet and shower and all that?"

He laughed. "Yes, this is not my first time being among your people. I spent time with humans when I was younger."

"Good, and don't even try relieving yourself outside. If someone catches you, even in this part of the world, they'll have you arrested, and it'll be difficult to explain to local law enforcement why I've got a naked seal man running around my yard."

Again, the man looked at me strangely, my attempt at humor apparently lost on him. This was harder than I expected, so I decided to take the bull by the horns and get to the bottom of his real reason for being here. I knew he'd told me he just needed a safe place to sleep, but all my Spidey senses were tingling, telling me there was a lot more to his story.

"Tell me what you want from me."

He looked down at his hands. "I don't want anything from you, at least not yet. I'm on a quest from the Council of Elders to find someone in particular. I'm still recovering from the injuries I sustained yesterday, although I'm in much better shape now thanks to you and your healing powers."

"So, you honestly just need a place to stay for a few days until you feel better?"

"Precisely," Muir said.

"And you want to be friends with benefits?" I asked. Again, he looked perplexed, and I couldn't help but laugh. "In other words, while you're here, you'd like to share my bed?"

The man smiled. "Mating, yes. If you are agreeable, I would like that very much."

I shrugged, but couldn't help grinning in return. "I don't mind that arrangement, as long as you don't try to force me into marriage or anything."

Muir laughed. "You are a strange human. It's almost like you're more afraid of me stealing your pelt than I am of you stealing mine."

"This is what a modern gay man looks like, my friend," I said, then got up and walked around the table before leaning down to kiss him.

I wasn't a fool. The man was beyond beautiful. I already knew what it felt like to have his body beneath me, moving in rhythm with mine. If he wanted to play around for a few days while getting himself well enough to face the deep blue sea again, who was I to argue?

When I pulled back from the kiss, Muir was smiling.

"Are you hungry?" I asked.

He nodded. "Yes, very. I would offer to go catch us a meal, but unfortunately, I'm not ready to go back into the sea just yet."

"Don't worry, I have fresh salmon, will that work for you?"

His eyes lit up. "Yes, please," he said. "I was chasing a large salmon when I was attacked. It's rare to find them in my part of the world any longer, so I was excited about having one all to myself."

I winked at him. "In that case, I'll cut up the entire fish. You're lucky, our laws limit how much salmon can be harvested, but my friend is an avid fisherman. He hates the taste, so he gave me half his catch and the rest to his mom."

I was about to start cooking when it struck me how he was likely accustomed to eating fish raw. "Do you prefer sushi, or do you mind if I cook it?"

"Sushi?" he asked, the word clearly foreign on his tongue, and I chuckled at how strange it sounded coming from him.

"Sorry. Do you prefer it raw or cooked?"

He considered that for a moment. "It's been a long time since I ate food cooked by humans. I'm afraid if I eat too much, it'll upset my stomach. Why don't you cook some and what you don't want, I'll take raw."

"That sounds like a perfect plan."

As a late lunch, I cooked my part of the fish with a mustard and raspberry glaze, the way I preferred it, while Muir ate his as sashimi.

I spent a season in Japan with my mom before she got sick, and although I was far from an expert, I'd learned how to slice salmon, so the texture was perfect. Instead of giving him a slab of the fish, I cut it into thin slices and placed it on a bed of ice while mine cooked.

I knew a harbor seal could eat up to ten pounds of salmon in one sitting, so I only cooked a small portion for myself, reserving most of the fish for him.

As we sat down, I laid out the food for us both and his eyes grew wide. "You gave me a very generous portion. I'm not sure I can eat all this."

I chuckled. "I apologize. I don't have a lot of experience feeding Selkie. I do study harbor seals, though, and I know they can put away a lot of fish."

The man looked at me sternly. "I'm *not* a harbor seal. We are our own species. In my seal form, I can eat many fish every day. In my human form, however, I can only eat smaller portions. Maybe you can freeze this in one of your electronic ice machines and save the rest for tomorrow."

"I've dedicated my life to studying harbor seals and hold them in high regard, but my apologies if the comparison caused offense. And yes, I can and will freeze whatever you don't eat."

That seemed to placate him, and he nodded. "Tell me, David, about your family in Ireland."

I sighed at the shift in conversation. I didn't spend much time with other people, other than work and occasionally, Marta, so I was out of practice. Unfortunately, this Selkie was more talkative than I expected. Although Muir had pointed out Selkie were their own species, I still anticipated some similarities between him and the seals I studied. But they clearly didn't extend to social interactions since harbor seals were quite solitary creatures and Muir seemed anything but.

"I don't know much about them, assuming I even have family still living there. As I said before, my great-grandmother was from Toraigh, and I went back several years ago to visit. I searched for relatives before and after my trip, but the only ones I could find lived here in the States. My great-grandmother immigrated to Tennessee before my grandma was born and, unfortunately, most of our connection to the old country died with her."

"Were they witches too?" he asked as if he were asking if we all had red hair. "Did they have the same powers you used to heal me?"

I choked. "No, we don't call that witch power. It's not widespread in my family, either. I seem to have gotten the majority of these... abilities."

"I see," he said, "...and your family lives inland?"

I laughed. "Yes, Tennessee is in the middle of the continent. It's where I grew up."

"But you felt compelled to be near the ocean?"

I continued smiling. "Yes, I love the ocean. I'm a marine biologist by trade, in part because I felt so drawn to the sea."

"Why not settle back in Ireland?" he asked.

"I don't mean to be rude, but you'd think I'd be the one with the questions."

He smiled. "I'm seeking someone on this quest, and fate has brought us together. I wondered if maybe you are the one I seek."

I laughed loudly this time. "Unless you're seeking someone who mostly wants his solitude, occasionally likes the company of another man, and prefers to spend his time studying marine life, I doubt I'm your guy."

He considered me for a long moment, before he said, "Yet you have very powerful magic. The Fae is strong in you."

I shook my head. Our conversation was getting stranger by the moment, so I decided to distract us from further weirdness by collecting the dishes and prepping the leftover food for tomorrow. As he said, I could freeze the salmon, so I wouldn't have to find fresh fish for him. I was thankful for that since fresh fish cost a fortune, and I was on a tight budget. Between my career as a marine biologist and leading whale-watching tours, I managed to keep myself afloat, but sometimes, just barely.

"Do you need a swim before you go to bed? The seawater might do you good."

The man looked at me strangely, but nodded. "It would help with the healing process, but I can't afford to take a chance with the Dorcha. That's what attacked me, and I'm not strong enough yet to fend one off if more are lurking."

"Dorcha?" I asked.

"Yes, sorry, it's Gaelic for dark entity."

"Well, you're in luck," I said happily. "We should be relatively safe in my lagoon. I'll throw my wet suit on and join you."

I quickly grabbed my wet suit and snorkel, and he followed me, pelt in hand, as we went down to the lagoon at the foot of the hill, not far from the cave. The lagoon was only open to the sea during the highest tide or King tide. As a result, I was confident any dark sea creatures wouldn't be able to reach us.

When we reached the beach, Muir's face bloomed. "I had no idea this was here. Usually, I can sense these pools."

I didn't want to promote the whole witch idea, but I felt a slight sense of pride at Muir's comment. I'd intuitively placed a barrier around the lagoon after moving here. Doing so made the place feel safer and more secluded, which I assured Muir of, so that he'd feel at least somewhat secure shifting out in the open.

He made short work of stripping out of the sweats and t-shirt, lifted the pelt over his head, and as the pelt came down over his body, his body rippled as he transformed into a seal. He was in the water before I had time to react. I stared after him shocked... I knew he was a magical creature, but I hadn't been prepared for him to show me just how magical he was. The transformation was quick and nothing like you would see on television. Basically, his human body disappeared as his seal body took over. I watched him play in the water and my scientific mind took note of the differences in him and harbor seals. His pelt was brown, more than grey and he was slightly bigger than most harbor seals. Had I encountered him in the wild, I'd have thought maybe he was some sort of hybrid species.

It took me significantly longer to don my wetsuit and get the snorkel in place so I could join him in the lagoon. I took a few moments to get my head on straight before diving in.

Thanks to Marta, I'd heard about and seen several magical creatures, yet my mind had trouble processing what I was seeing as Muir shifted. It was almost like I could accept he was human, or a seal, but I couldn't quite accept he was both.

I kept my distance as he played in the deeper part of the lagoon. I probably would've swam there with him if he were a wild animal instead of a human-animal hybrid.

There were, unfortunately, no fish left in the lagoon. By the time the water was warm enough to swim in, whatever sea life had gotten caught in the pool during a King tide had died due to lack of food or oxygen. Anything left alive was either microscopic, tidepool shellfish, or crabs.

Mostly, I used the lagoon as a way to study the waters themselves. I'd written several papers about how the organisms progressed throughout the year. Like now, there were quite a few still living, but by late summer, when the pool was warm enough to swim in without the wet suit, it would be almost sterile.

My research, although obscure, had been used in several larger projects to explain how species were forced to evolve when great seas shifted and became isolated. I'd even been pulled into a project studying the Black Sea and one about the lochs of Scotland.

I tired of swimming much sooner than Muir and pulled myself out of the water. I went to the small makeshift shed I'd erected when I first moved here and changed into shorts.

The spring sun was starting to set, and not having slept much the night before, I grabbed the old blanket I kept in the shed for just this type of occasion, spread it out across the sand, and closed my eyes while soaking up the last rays of sunshine.

I awoke sometime later to find the sexy man lying next to me on the blanket. I smiled at him. "Did you have a nice swim?" I asked.

He nodded. "It was just what I needed, thanks."

"Good, I'm glad," I said, and stretched luxuriously in the sun's fading light.

# Seven

## Muir

David was a strange man. I could sense he felt wary of me while I swam in the lagoon, but I guessed it was because he knew wild animals needed distance. I never sensed any fear, though, nor did he seem uncomfortable when I changed form in front of him.

He'd argued with me that he wasn't a witch, which confused me. I understood keeping such things a secret from other humans, but he'd healed me, used his powers to give me strength, and didn't fear or shy away from me as a Fae being. All of those things indicated that he was indeed a witch, and a powerful one.

Regardless, I decided to let the subject drop. I enjoyed this human. He was different, odd, accepting, and very physically appealing. I looked forward to mating with him often.

That night, however, after we climbed back up to his dwelling, he didn't mate with me again. Instead, I was placed in the lonely room away from his. I was disappointed. It had been many months since I'd had a mate, and our intimate acts in the cave had only whetted my appetite. Regardless, I didn't let it dissuade me.

Surprisingly, I fell asleep quickly. When I'd been among humans before, it took me many long, restless nights to get used to sleeping in beds. They were squishy and often made my back hurt, but that wasn't the case here.

David's energy permeated the home, his power a slow, steady hum, not unlike a heartbeat. The rhythm reminded me of the sea, which resulted in me sleeping soundly.

The next morning, I woke to unidentifiable noises outside my room. The sun wasn't quite up, but David's energy pulsated slightly faster than it had during the night. I climbed out of bed and went in search of him.

I found him in the kitchen, making something with a small machine I'd never seen before. The smell emanating from it accosted my senses.

"Good morning," David said when he saw me. "Would you like coffee?"

I eyed the brown liquid dripping steadily inside the machine. If the pungent aroma was any indication, drinking it would not be pleasurable. "No, thank you."

He appeared amused as he poured himself a cup. "So, what drink would you like?" he asked.

"Hmm. I do like something called *fuisce*."

David shrugged. "I'm not sure what that is. It sounds Gaelic, though. I could try to figure out if we have it here."

"Whisky. I heard it called that once."

David laughed. "Yes, we definitely have that. You really are from Ireland."

"Nay." I shook my head as I sat down at the kitchen table. "I'm from Scotland, officially. Our people no longer occupy the Irish lands. It's too dangerous. We mostly live north of Scotland, in the North and Norwegian Seas."

"Fewer people?" he asked.

"Yes, that's the main reason. We also prefer the cooler waters. Fewer predators lurk there, and we have protections in place against the Dorcha, who aren't allowed to enter our waters."

David came to sit across the table from me, sipping his coffee. "I've heard legends of the Selkie, but never the Dorcha. What are they?"

"I'm not surprised you don't know of them. Do you know the history of the Fae?" I asked.

He chuckled. "You mean like fairies?"

"Yes, like the Fair Folk."

"Oh, you're serious? I've heard legends of them, but it's not like I ever took much stock."

I didn't understand what he meant by not taking stock, but since his knowledge of the Fae was lacking, I decided to teach him what even the youngest Selkie knew.

"The Fae lived in the northern reaches of what you call Europe even before the large ice sheets spread across the lands. When humans began to venture into their territory, they were intrigued, eventually intermingling and interbreeding with them. Unfortunately, humans don't play well with others, and they procreate a great deal faster than the Fae, so it didn't take long before humans significantly outnumbered pureblooded Fae."

David looked at me quizzically, his forehead scrunched, and eyebrows furrowed as if confused. I almost laughed at how easily he seemed to handle my transforming into a seal but accepting this true tale challenged him. I decided to reverse course and take a different tack.

"Why do you think you have powers other humans don't?" I asked.

He shrugged and took a long sip of his coffee. "I honestly don't know. I'm not sure anyone really knows."

"Well, there's a simple explanation. You have Fae ancestors. Not just a few, you have several."

He choked on his coffee and rushed to grab a paper towel to wipe himself off before returning to the table.

"I seriously doubt my ancestors were fairies," he said.

"It isn't something to doubt, David. It simply is. You have both Fae and human ancestors. Over the generations, several Fae must've joined your direct human family line to keep the power inside you as strong as it is." Before he could dismiss me, I continued. "I have both human and Fae blood within me. My ancestors, however, were sea-based Fae. In fact, an entire tribe mixed with some of the first humans to arrive in northern Europe. That's why we are Selkie."

"And the Dorcha?" he asked. "Are they related to you?"

"Yes, the Dorcha were once Selkie as well. When the humans became more hostile, a faction within our tribe who were less accepting of their human side wanted to fight them. Of course, the Fae Queen forbade it. The Fae intuitively knew fighting the humans was a losing proposition. Unfortunately, the Dorcha ancestors ignored the Queen and went to war. The battles were intense, and many humans died. Even now, human stories like *Beowulf* describe Dorcha who came on land to destroy humanity."

David's eyebrow cocked as I said that, and I could tell he wanted to challenge me, but I didn't want to argue with him. Humans were notoriously ignorant of the history of early human movements. If he was the man I sought, I needed him to understand, so he had time to come to terms with his place in the ongoing situation.

"The Fae Queen was set to punish all Selkie for disobeying her, but the Selkie leaders begged her to recognize not all of our people were guilty. That day, she cursed the Dorcha with an inability to function outside the ocean, though they can transform into any sea creature. The curse also made them weaker than humans, especially those who have the Fae gift. So, they mostly avoid humans now."

"But they don't avoid you?"

I shook my head sadly. "No, they are now the enemy of all Selkie. Mostly, I think it's jealousy and anger for their kin who turned against them. Regardless, after years of warfare, both Selkie and Dorcha populations were painfully low. As the Romans began to leave the British Isles, we reached an agreement. Selkie would remain in the northern reaches of the Atlantic, and the Dorcha would occupy the rest."

"That doesn't seem fair. The oceans are vast, and you gave that over to them?"

"I didn't. This was over a thousand years before I was born."

David narrowed his eyes and looked me up and down, as if trying to decipher something. "Just how old are you?"

I laughed. "I'm coming into my twenty-eighth year. We live longer than humans, but we age the same otherwise."

"Do the Dorcha age the same as well?"

"No, thank the goddess, and they reproduce much slower, like our Fae ancestors."

David sat quietly, appearing to absorb all I'd said. "You said witches, as you called me, are descended from the Fae?"

I nodded. "Yes, but not just the northern Fae. Most human witches are descended from the Fae who occupied the deserts of Africa. At one time, the Sahara Desert, as you call it, was lush and green. The southern Fae lived in those jungles. Their magic was similar to the northern Fae, but it was more earth and fire based. Or you could be descended from the Fae who occupied what's now called Asia. Far less is known about them, at least by our Elders."

"So, all of those Fae intermingled with humans too?" David asked.

"Yes, especially in Africa. As the deserts took over the jungles, the Fae began to die off. They were too powerfully linked with the land to survive. The only way they could was to interbreed with the humans who'd recently begun to move into that region."

We were getting too deep, and I felt that if I continued with too much information, I'd lose him altogether. Before changing the subject, I thought for a few moments, concentrating on what I needed him to know.

"The Fae of the north and east combined forces and transitioned out of this dimension. They chose to retreat instead of facing the ongoing wars against the rising human populations." I could see more questions forming in David's mind, so to distract him, I leaned across the table and kissed his lips. "That's enough history for today," I said. "I may tell you more later, but for now, just know you and I aren't that different."

"And the Dorcha aren't that different from us either?" he asked, and I cringed.

"We are all related, but we have very different goals in life," I said. "Now, I'm starving. Shall we finish off that salmon?"

"I have a better idea. There's a great sushi place in town. Why don't I treat you to several different seafood options besides salmon? We can save the frozen stuff for later."

I liked the sound of that since in seal form, I loved having my choice of different fish or shellfish, not to mention, it meant spending more time with David.

# Eight

## David

Despite my best efforts to maintain boundaries, I was becoming attached to my visitor. He was almost always serious, which wasn't all too surprising considering he was, in many ways, a wild animal. Life could be very serious when spending copious amounts of time trying not to be discovered by humans, natural predators, or Dorcha.

I had the unexplainable urge to make him laugh, or at least prod him a bit until I got a reaction.

I shouldn't take his story about all magical people and creatures being descended from the Fae at face value, though it made for one hell of a tale. The idea I was the essentially the same as him was even harder to swallow.

As we got into my car to head to the sushi place, I was concerned the drive to town might overwhelm him. But he rolled the window down and enjoyed the wind as it blew across his face. I glanced over at him and almost swallowed my tongue.

Long dark hair flowed in the breeze and fell across his pale, delicate features. His intensely dark eyebrows and eyelashes made him look otherworldly. *Actually*, I thought, *considering he is, why am I surprised?*

Seeing him content and happy caused a strange sensation to settle in the pit of my stomach. I knew I was attracted to him, my desire couldn't be denied, but I didn't usually feel this intensely about hookups.

Sure, I'd fooled around, but I hadn't seriously dated a man since my undergrad program at the University of Tennessee. I quickly learned I didn't like relationships very much and preferred a solitary lifestyle over so-called domestic bliss.

I let out a deep sigh as I thought about that. Sometimes I regretted not wanting to share my life with someone. My mom, stepfather, and grandparents had all been well-suited to married life. Even my stepbrother was now firmly attached to my sister-in-law.

Something was clearly wrong with me, and I never entirely understood it. I'd get to like someone, try to get close to them, then doubts would fill my mind and before I knew it, I'd kick them out of my life for good.

Muir must've heard my sigh, because he turned to me, smiling. "I've forgotten how exhilarating it is to ride in one of these machines."

It was eye-opening to be around someone with so little access to things I took for granted, like cars. It reminded me just how incredibly different our life experiences were, even when in his human form.

"Do you have to dodge boats and ships?" I asked him out of the blue, because thinking about cars made me wonder about shipping routes.

His smile faded as he nodded. "It's becoming more and more dangerous as the years go on. When the barrier was at its strongest, few humans came into our territories. They were naturally repelled from our hunting areas and where we swam." He looked off into the distance before shaking his head. "In the past decade, we've suffered numerous casualties as shipping and boating activity increased around us. That's one of the reasons I was sent on my quest."

I'd honestly forgotten about his quest, as he'd called it, which made me feel bad. "Tell me more about this quest. Why are you seeking some witch to save you?"

Muir looked at me with contempt. "The legend is not very old, certainly not as old as the one where the Dorcha and Selkie were forever separated. That doesn't make it any less valid, however."

I pulled up to the restaurant and parked the car near the front door.

"I can tell you the story while we eat.," he said, looking toward the building. "Shall we go order first?"

"You've been to a restaurant before then?" I asked.

He nodded, a wide grin returning to his face. "Yes, many times while I was on my *coisich mun cuairth.*"

"Your what? I asked, my eyebrows going up at his lapse into Gaelic.

"Oh, it's what we call our walkabout. When young Selkie come of age and venture ashore to spend time with our land cousins."

"Cool," I said, shrugging, "...then let's go. I'm starving!"

Muir seemed right at home as we entered the restaurant and were seated. He looked around, smiling at the sea decor. The sushi here wasn't traditional Japanese. A man from Japan had married into the family that owned the restaurant, and they'd integrated sushi rolls and other dishes into the menu decades before. The result was often eclectic meal combinations.

When the menu was placed in front of Muir, he frowned. "I'm sorry, David, but I don't read. I tried to learn while I was on my *coisich mun cuairth*, but my understanding of written words remains limited. Do you mind ordering for me?" he asked. "I would enjoy a *fuisce*, though."

"No problem," I whispered, leaning in close to him. "I'm sure you don't have much need for written languages in the ocean, but it's very handy here on land. Maybe I can teach you while you're stuck here with me."

I was not sure why I offered. Surely he wouldn't be with me long enough to teach him to read. I was beginning to feel like maybe I'd gotten myself into more than I was willing to handle.

"Anyway," I quickly added to change the subject, "...if you've never had sake, I'd like you to try it. It's like whisky but made from rice instead of barley."

Muir nodded, but still looked confused as he tried to decipher the menu. Finally, the server came back over, and I ordered for each of us. Muir was still staring at the menu when I'd finished, so I told the server to come back later. We might want dessert.

Muir looked up. "Oh, did the serving wench want my menu?" he asked, and I flinched.

"Um, that word means something very different here than where you're from."

"Really?" he asked. "It wasn't that long since I did my *coisich mun cuairth*."

"Yes, but this is the United States, not northern Scotland, if that's where you did your coisch... thing," I said, giving up on trying to pronounce it.

He chuckled. "*Coisich mun cuairth*. I did my walkabout in Scotland. We tend to stick to areas our ancestors lived. Being close to the old Fae sites is good for us and helps center us for our lives at sea."

"So, back to the point, in the US, wench usually means a prostitute. Someone who sells their body... mates, for money."

"And that is bad?" he asked.

I laughed loud enough to turn some heads, but kept my voice down as I spoke. "Yes, that's very bad here. It's considered very improper and it's illegal as well."

"I see. Land humans have a strange relationship with mating. We tend just to enjoy intimacy and not assign so much meaning to it."

"I'm more like that myself, but you probably shouldn't call our server a wench unless you want her to do nasty things to your food."

Muir's eyes grew big at that. "Do you think she'd poison us?"

I shook my head. "No, but she might spit on your food."

Muir didn't get it, I could tell, and I smiled at his innocence. I silently wondered if I would be the same if our tables were turned. Not that I could ever be in his world. I might enjoy sushi and the sea, but I still just had two legs, after all.

# NINE

## MUIR

THE DRIVE BACK TO David's dwelling was quiet. I could tell he was in a playful mood, but for whatever reason, he kept his thoughts to himself.

David was different from other humans I'd encountered. I wondered if maybe that was because he was a witch. I'd listened to the Elders tell stories about how witches, including the Dion Adair's mother, had been persecuted through the ages. The half-Selkie leader had encouraged the Selkie to learn the written languages of the lands we occupied, but few did. By and large, the old stories were told to us as we sat on beaches, resting between swims.

Most Selkie weren't interested in learning more than the most basic human skills. Doing so required being out of the water when they were young, a time in life when shedding one's pelt was most difficult. I'd been willing to resist the call of the ocean to learn. Humans had and still fascinated me more than most of my people. I also knew that one day, based on Merrow's visions, my quest would require I possess such knowledge.

That said, I hadn't spent time with humans since I returned to the sea years ago. Being around David now, though, I regretted not having studied harder in order to feel more adept in his world.

Deep in thought, I wasn't paying attention when we began to cross a bridge spanning a river that flowed into the ocean. I startled when David slammed on his brakes, but I only had to look up to see why. A giant octopus clung to the bridge, blocking our passage.

"Enteroctopus dofleini, out of the water?" David said in astonishment, mostly to himself. When he started to get out of the car, I reached over to stop him.

"No, it's Dorcha," I said sharply, which snapped him out of his wonderment.

"How can you tell?" he asked, perplexed.

"Use your senses, not your eyes," I said, encouraging him.

David paused and I watched as his body flinched the moment he felt the intense anger flowing from the creature.

"What do we do now?"

Unsure how to advise him, I silently cursed myself for being so unprepared. I had relied too heavily on the Dion Adair's stone for guidance, and now that the sapphire was gone, I was at a loss in more ways than one. "If I were in the ocean, I'd swim away or draw other creatures to help me, but I'm not sure what to do on land."

David's eyebrows knitted as he sat staring at the Dorcha. "I may have an idea."

When he opened the car door, I stopped him again. "No, you have no idea what else awaits you. It's best to turn around and wait it out. It may just be passing through."

"What if some other person comes upon the creature? They won't hesitate to get out. We can't knowingly put unsuspecting people in danger like that."

"More Dorcha are near, I can feel them, David. Can't you?"

He shook his head. "No, I can only feel... anger, but not from who or how many."

"You should practice your craft," I admonished, frustrated with him and myself that we were so ill-prepared to handle the situation. "Can you move things with your mind?"

"Some, but not with much control."

"Some is better than none. You must move the Dorcha, or run over it. Either way, we can't face these creatures alone."

David closed his eyes, and I watched as perspiration began to bead his forehead. I looked out, and the giant octopus hadn't budged.

"I can't move it. I'm not strong enough."

"No, David, you are. You healed me and my pelt. That takes more power than moving a creature off the road and back into the ocean."

Just then, the car began to move. I felt a great presence under the bridge and knew several Dorcha were below us, and the swaying was somehow related to the bridge and its infrastructure.

Dorcha were powerful creatures, and I had no doubt the integrity of the bridge was no match for them, especially as they gathered in numbers below us. I could only assume they were trying to upset its balance and effectively toss us into the water.

"David, we have to move. Go, now."

"I can't just kill it."

"Even if that means it will kill us?"

David's mouth gaped open and shut like a fish when another idea came to mind. Could my limited powers help David focus his?

I grabbed David's hand and yelled for him to concentrate. I felt his powers connect instantly with mine and couldn't help the sigh that escaped. Having David's powers surge inside me felt the same as when we'd mated. Light and color mixed in my mind, causing an almost erotic experience.

When the car lurched to the right, I woke up from the hypnotic energy and yelled, "Push your energy into the creature. Force him over the bridge."

Without hesitation, David did as I instructed, and within moments, the giant octopus leaped from the bridge and into the water below.

The Dorcha screamed in unison, the high-pitched screech of my enemies ripping at my ears.

David yelped at the sound, alerting me to the fact that he, too, could hear them. Then, before I knew what was happening, he grabbed a lever and pushed it sharply down as the car lurched forward across the bridge and back onto land.

I could feel other Dorcha around us, but they hadn't been as brave as the octopus. Not yet, at least. I knew instinctively that would change. When I'd first reached this part of the ocean, I felt the presence of Dorcha, but they were few. That had changed since the one had attacked me.

The number of Dorcha under the bridge had been more than I'd ever encountered. Gathering in such large numbers indicated they knew of my quest and were actively trying to stop me. The situation was only becoming more dangerous, for myself and now David, and I needed to figure out how to safely depart this place as quickly as possible. The real question, though, was how to convince David to come with me.

David

I hadn't expected to see a giant Pacific octopus straddling the bridge between my place and town, and when I had, I was immediately concerned it had been injured. Had Muir not stopped me, I would've gotten out to check.

The moment I concentrated my energy on the creature, I knew what Muir had said was true. An intense anger pulsed from the creature, much sharper than the dark energy I'd sensed from the Dorcha that had attacked Muir. I'd never had any direct contact with Dorcha in the past, or if I had, I didn't know it. So why did that one hate me so much? Maybe it thought I was part of Muir's quest.

Regardless of the reason, I kept the gas pedal floored the rest of the way back to my place. Between Marta's protective shields and mine, I figured my home was the safest place to be for the time being.

When we pulled up to the cottage, and before I opened the car door, I asked Muir if he sensed anything sinister around us.

Muir looked at me shyly. "Um, no. They were concentrated around the bridge."

I nodded. "Yeah, that's what I thought. I can't feel them either."

I was about to get out when I noticed the strange look on Muir's face hadn't changed. "Um, are you okay?" I asked.

"No. I'm no longer safe here, and I'm also putting you in danger." He sighed deeply, then climbed out of the car.

He didn't speak as we walked into the cottage. I began to follow him toward the guest room, but decided to leave him alone. I was unsure how to manage what had to be a lot of fear on his part and, unfortunately, there wasn't much I could do to help the situation anyway.

I put the kettle on, grabbed the herbal tea I kept for cold nights, and sat at the table to ponder all that'd happened. When Muir had grabbed my hand on the bridge, I felt so much of his spirit pour into me. It was sexual, but more than that, it was... I shook my head. It wasn't like anything I'd ever experienced before. It was almost as if our minds had connected.

When the kettle boiled, I got up to make the tea. Just as I was about to sit back down, I heard a knock at the door.

I glanced at my clock to see it was well past nine. I was afraid it might be the Dorcha coming to attack. "Muir, we've got company," I said quietly as I knocked on his door.

"They are human," he responded without coming out.

"Okay," I said, and decided we were probably alright.

When I opened my door, I was surprised to see my annoyed-looking friend staring at me. "Have you not learned anything from our lessons?" she asked.

"Um, Marta?" I asked.

"Yeah, Marta," she said. "Now move out of the way. I can feel you have a magical creature in your home."

"Magic... wait, how do you know?"

"'Cause I practice my gift, you nitwit," she muttered as she irritably shoved past me. Marta never spoke to me that way, so I knew she was more than a little upset.

"I just made myself some herbal tea, can I get you some?"

"First, you introduce me to..." She lifted her head as if she were sniffing and looked around the room. "Is it a Selkie you have in here?"

I grinned at the thought of the sexy man currently occupying my guest room. "Yeah, but he's sort of depressed right now. So, I think we should leave him alone. We've had quite the day."

She eyed me for a long moment, then sighed. "You've gone and fallen in love with a Selkie, haven't you? Why is he here? This is a long way from where he should be."

"Marta, that's a long story."

"One I'm happy to tell. Greetings, witch. I am Muir Fen, head warrior of the Fair Isle clan. You may call me Muir."

"Greetings to you, Muir. I'm Marta Malone. Have you been trapped here by my over-amorous friend?"

Muir chuckled. "No, he's never tried to force me to stay."

"Then, may I ask why you're here?"

Muir quickly told Marta about the Dorcha attack and me saving him in the cave. When he mentioned I'd healed his pelt as well, Marta looked surprised. "Well, you have been listening. Good, then I won't be angry with you any longer. Now, I'll gladly take you up on that tea."

Muir and Marta were instant friends, much to my chagrin. I didn't say a word as the two chatted and got to know one another. As I made Marta's tea, Muir filled her in on all that had happened, minus our sexual exploits, of course.

But I knew my friend well enough to know she was already aware of all that. If Marta knew one thing above all others, it was when people developed feelings for each other. That ability had gone a long way in helping support her too. Her little shop on the Oregon coast, where she offered her brand of fortune-telling among other things, brought in a great deal of money. The locals all called her the love witch, which she relished and did everything she could to promote it.

When I brought the tea to the living room, Marta patted the seat next to her, encouraging me to sit down. It always shocked me, even after all these years, how Marta took ownership of every room she entered. I just shook my head and sat on the sofa.

"There was so much negative energy coming from this direction that I closed my shop early to get here. What was that about?"

Muir sighed. "The Dorcha are tracking me. Usually, if a Selkie goes ashore, the Dorcha give up, but it seems the one on the bridge brought reinforcements instead."

"Tell me more about that," she demanded.

I let Muir tell the story and only interrupted when he talked about how the octopus had been too big to be natural. After I explained that it was, in fact, standard size for a giant Pacific octopus, he sighed with relief. "So, they haven't acquired magical powers outside their own."

Marta reached into her purse and pulled out a small stone that glowed slightly. "This is a very powerful object," she said as she handed the stone to Muir. "I found it on the bridge where I assume you met the Dorcha, since I sensed dark energy lingering there. Have you ever seen this before?"

Muir gasped. "It's the Dion Adair's stone," he said, clutching it to his chest. "The Dorcha must've found it near the cave and then lost it when we tossed him back into the water."

"It's important to you, then?" she asked, her head slightly tilted as if she were piecing together a puzzle.

"It is," he said.

Muir looked into my eyes just as his glazed over for a moment. I felt a rush of energy flow from me to him, and I knew something important had just happened.

When Muir looked down at the blue sapphire in his hand, he nodded to himself. "I've found the one I've been seeking," he said.

"Explain," Marta prompted him.

He hesitated for a moment. "The message I've come to deliver is meant only for the Dion Adair, our protector, to hear. But you are his teacher, so I see no reason not to share it with you as well." He took a deep breath, before continuing, "The Selkie are in grave danger. Humans have begun encroaching on all the places we once occupied with little to no threat. We suffer increasing casualties each year from more ships accessing our fishing grounds. David also confirmed the climate is changing, which we have long suspected. We have felt the seas growing warmer, and fish are no longer as plentiful as they once were because of it."

He hesitated again as if trying to figure out how much to share. I could see when he decided to finally come clean. "There was an original Dion Adair who was half-witch, half-Selkie. After his parents were burned at the stake, he left his siblings to live with the Selkie, using his father's pelt to transform into a Selkie himself."

Marta sat on the edge of the sofa and prompted him to go on. Muir nodded. "The Dion Adair placed magical barriers around the Selkie safe holdings, but recently those protections have begun to break down. The Dion Adair understood this would happen and predicted that a day would come when we would need to seek out a child descended from one of his siblings. One who possessed the powerful witch skills he had."

Muir looked to me then, and Marta followed his gaze with wide eyes. "Wait. You... you think that's me?" I asked, and immediately stood up.

"I suspected it, yes, and now that your teacher has returned the stone, I know..."

"No," I interrupted. "I don't want to be part of this fanciful legend, so don't start putting this mumbo jumbo on me. I'm a scientist who knows some glorified parlor tricks, not a witch. Marta, you go help him!" I stomped out of the cottage and down the path to the lagoon, my true safe haven.

Before I reached the beach, I thrust out my energy to detect any evil presence lurking nearby. When I could tell the coast was clear, I proceeded to my little shed, grabbed the old blanket and folding chair stored inside, and plunked myself down in front of it. I'd built the shed for nights such as this, when I needed to be alone with my thoughts.

Anger filled me, almost to the point of rage. I knew it was irrational, but it was like the same darkness that had radiated from the Dorcha earlier was bursting out of me now. And I let it come.

All the questions about my background and heritage began to make sense now, not that the realization brought any comfort. Muir was setting me up to be some freaking hero in a comic book, and I wasn't having it. I bet the fucking stone was just a prop to seal the deal. No, I wouldn't fucking play. I had no desire to be someone's hero. I wanted a simple life, taking tourists out to see the whales, studying the habitat in my lagoon, and living in my cottage on the high cliffs overlooking the Pacific. That was all I wanted, nothing else.

Wasn't that why I'd moved halfway across the country? I controlled my own destiny, not my stepfather, not my new friend with benefits, and certainly not some old Selkie lore. And I'd be damned if I'd fall for these theatrics, no matter how connected I felt with Muir. For all I cared, he could take his damned pelt and swim off into the fucking sunset, alone.

# TEN

— · —

## MUIR

"T HAT WENT WELL," MARTA, David's witch friend, said.

I looked at her oddly, unsure what she meant. There was no denying I had screwed things up badly. If I'd had the stone when I first met David, I would've known. I could've given him the speech I'd practiced over and over as I swam across the Atlantic, through the canal and up the Pacific coast, and finally here, where the stone had led me.

Instead, I'd made a total mess of things, and David probably thought I'd set him up. How would I ever convince him now?

"How did it go well? David is clearly upset with me."

Marta chuckled. "Listen, Muir, David isn't what you'd call fond of his magical abilities. In fact, he only allowed me to help when his powers began getting out of control."

"That explains why he was so shocked when I called him a witch when we met."

Marta leaned back on the sofa and laughed. "Oh, I'm sure he hated that."

I blushed. "I-I didn't mean to offend him."

"You didn't, sweetheart, but you'll have to give him a little space," she said. "I'll tell you a secret. I felt your arrival and almost came up here then, but the spirits held me back. David is notorious for loving his men and leaving them. He's not one to take a lover for very long, let alone have heart-eyes. However, the way I saw him looking at you tonight..."

That caught me by surprise. "Surely you are wrong. David has been clear from the start. He has no feelings for me, and when it's time for me to leave, he'll be happy to see me go. Apparently, that time has come, but I can't leave now knowing he is indeed the one I seek."

Marta reached over and patted my knee. "That's his defenses. I can see he's already developed feelings for you, Muir. And from what you've told me, it appears that may all be part of your and his fate. Although, for the goddess's sake, never tell him that." Marta shook her head and let out a long sigh. "If he ever thinks this is a fate thing, he'll reject it as fast as he can. David isn't one to tolerate anyone or anything forcing him to do something. He's a stubborn man, that one. But as you have already guessed, he's also a special one."

I nodded. I'd begun having feelings for the man the moment I woke up in that cave with his body pressed against mine to keep warm. He'd taken care of me, but he'd also taken care of my pelt, which showed he valued both sides of me.

Marta finished her tea and stood to take the cup into David's kitchen. I sat and thought about him until she returned. "There is nothing to do tonight. David will stay down at his lagoon and pout. You sleep in his bed, and I'll take the guest room. I'm sure tomorrow he'll be better able to digest what you have to say to him."

I nodded and thought she was probably telling the truth, considering she knew him much better than me. The lagoon felt like David, and I could tell it was his sanctuary. Even as I swam there, it was as much his energy that filled me as it was the energy from the water. Now that the stone had confirmed my suspicions, I could clearly see all the small clues I hadn't acknowledged before.

The energy around the lagoon was, in fact, the same energy as the barriers the original Dion Adair had erected around the Selkie territory. David was the man I sought, I knew that for a fact now, and I would do whatever necessary to ensure he returned with me to save our people. Even if it meant I had to sacrifice myself to do so.

# Eleven

—·—

## David

I woke up looking directly at a giant full moon. I'd dreamed of demons swimming in the oceans on the other side of the cliffs that created the lagoon and knew they were real. Something about their anger matched my own, and that scared me.

Muir was real as well—a Selkie who'd come seeking the savior of his people. No matter how I tried to rationalize it, I couldn't see myself as that hero. I'd read my share of fantasy novels, my choice of reading material growing up and in college, and I didn't resemble any of those heroes.

Strong, selfless, willing to sacrifice everything for whatever cause they were after. That wasn't me, couldn't be me. I was the opposite. Hell, I'd selfishly moved far from Tennessee to get away from what was left of my family. Not that my stepfather or stepsiblings had even noticed or cared, but still.

I'd deliberately bought the first isolated cottage I could afford on the Pacific coast and was lucky that the tourism business here was enough to keep me afloat financially. That was a pattern in my life. Leap first, deal with the consequences later.

I was certainly no fantasy novel hero. Hell, I was barely even a tolerable human being.

I thought of the darkness I could feel even now. No, I wasn't like the Dorcha either. I didn't hate humans, as those creatures did, but I was definitely a loner. Marta was one of only a few people I allowed into my life. My mom's cousins, who lived closer than the rest of my family, occasionally visited, but even they knew to keep their visits short.

I stared at the beautiful moon, and it was as if I could hear her asking, "But that's different with Muir, isn't it?"

I sighed. People had worshiped the goddess in the moon since humanity first walked the earth. I'd never given sway to religion one way or the other, but I answered her anyway. "Yes," I admitted aloud, "Yes, it's different with Muir."

"And why do you think that's the case?" she asked, the voice clearly echoing in my head.

"Because..." My mind went blank as I thought about it. "I don't know, he's just different."

I could hear humor in her voice, which sounded a lot like my great-grandmother's. "Figure out why it's different." Then her tone became serious. "Many lives depend on you, Dion Adair. And just as many intend to keep you from answering your calling." Images of my birth father flashed through my mind, then disappeared just as quickly.

Ignoring the random memories, I sighed. "But I'm not this Dion Adair. I'm no one's hero."

"No hero thinks of themselves as such. All creatures are called to different purposes, and this is yours. Given to you because of your skills and abilities. You are the only one yet... Whether you help the Selkie or turn your back is entirely your choice."

The voice disappeared and the next thing I remembered was waking up. It was still early morning. The moon and my conversation with the goddess had been a dream, but even in my stubbornness, I knew it'd been more.

I sighed and got up, folding the blanket and chair, and returned them to the shed. Then I began the climb up the path to the cottage, guessing it was time to face my future, whatever that might be.

# TWELVE

## MUIR

I HEARD TALKING AND knew David must've returned from the lagoon. I had barely slept, worried I'd jeopardized the entire quest, but not only that, I'd upset David. I was not sure how I could've done it differently, though. And now, I questioned whether or not I was the right person for this job. Perhaps Merrow had misidentified me in her long-ago vision. Maybe if I could get David to come to the Selkie homeland, someone more appropriate could take over. Someone who hadn't let his attraction for the Dion Adair distract him from saving his people.

I left the bedroom and kept my head down as I walked to where Marta and David were sitting at his kitchen table. They stopped talking when I entered the kitchen, and I decided this was my chance to apologize.

"I'm very sorry for the way I revealed all of this to you, David. I never meant to cause alarm or distress."

When I looked up, David was smiling. "Muir, you didn't do anything wrong. It was just a shock, but now that I've had some time to think about it, I'm not as upset. Marta has also been talking to me about how I can help."

"That's good," I said, and looked at the witch woman. "How do you see him helping?"

She smiled, but spoke in a serious tone, "You need the barriers rebuilt, which David can do. It's not like he'll have to take an epic journey back to your homeland either. Modern transportation will make the trip much quicker and easier for you both."

I wasn't sure what she meant, but decided it was best to let the second Dion Adair and his teacher devise their plan. They would need whatever witch powers they could bring to the situation anyway, since there was a debate over whether the Dion Adair's pelt would even work for someone whose bloodline was so diluted. It was best to keep that little detail to myself.

"I can't swim from here. There are too many Dorcha in these waters and their numbers are increasing. I can feel them gathering, waiting for me, even from here."

"Yes," Marta said. "I can feel them as well. But lucky for you, we have cars, airplanes, and all sorts of transportation to get you home."

"Overland," I said, unable to hide my disdain at having to leave the coast. I'd never been far away from the ocean. I wasn't even sure a Selkie could survive long without open water nearby.

"I'm not sure I can travel that far inland," I said honestly.

"You may have to try," Marta said. "Given what you told me last night about the Dorcha almost compromising the integrity of the bridge, they would have no problem upsetting a ship. So, that leaves us land and air travel."

"I'll have to travel as a human anyway, Muir," David told me. "I can't swim the ocean like you do."

I hadn't considered that—another mark against me. I'd been overconfident when I departed my homeland, armed with the Dion Adair's stone–which, thankfully, once again hung around my neck–and the full backing of the Council of Elders, but neither could help me now. I'd only planned on finding the second Dion Adair and convincing him to return with me. I hadn't even considered he wouldn't be able to travel through open water alongside me. If my warriors could see me now, they'd be shaking their heads at my lack of strategy and preparation.

"I suppose we have no choice," I conceded, despite my concern about being away from the ocean for too long.

"I have an idea," Marta said and looked at David. "But it'll require help."

David sighed. "You're finally luring me to your magic hippie village, aren't you?"

Marta smiled. "You knew it would happen eventually."

I was confused. I didn't know what a hippie village was, nor did I understand why David wanted to avoid it, but if visiting there could help me fulfill my quest, I was more than willing to go.

# Thirteen

## David

CHEMEKETA WAS AS MY stepfather's family would've said, "smaller than a gnat's ass," just a handful of shops surrounded by a few houses and a community building called the Grange House.

I'd driven through the tiny village not long after meeting Marta, because she told me I should get to know the locals, but even just driving by, people walking on both sides of the street looked at me strangely and I knew they could sense I had abilities, so I didn't stop. Instead, I drove through the town, turned around at the beach, and left, never to return.

I didn't need a whole community of people in the middle of my business. Whether or not they possessed similar abilities had little to do with it. That, in my mind, was just another reason to avoid the place.

Marta had been harassing me ever since to go back and give the place and the people a chance. "No," I responded every time. "You are more than enough magical woo-woo for me."

This time, however, I knew Marta was right. Unfortunately, I didn't understand or practice my skills enough to help Muir and his people in the ways they needed, not yet. I barely remembered the basics she'd shown me, which had jeopardized Muir when I first met him. I needed more help and training if I were to pull this off.

I locked up my cottage and, with Marta's help, reinforced the boundary shields she'd helped me build a few years earlier. It didn't really keep people away, and if someone wanted to rob me, it wouldn't stop them, but it did cause people who I didn't readily welcome to feel uneasy.

We decided to take an inland road to Chemeketa. It meant adding time to the trip, but after last night's run-in with the Dorcha, none of us wanted to take the chance of a repeat encounter. The moment we drove away my home, following Marta, a blast of negative energy hit us.

"Damn," I said, and looked over at Muir. "There's a lot of them out there now."

He nodded, looking pale. "I hope this witch village is able to help. My defenses are no match against this many Dorcha."

I reached over and laid my hand on his. He was clearly nervous, and I detected a shiver when my fingers grazed his. But just like the night before, the moment our hands touched, it was as if our energies merged, and I could feel him calming.

I kept my hand on his or vice versa the entire drive to Chemeketa. Something had shifted between us, and we were somehow connected in a more significant way, in an almost spiritual way. By the time we arrived in the village, several people were waiting for us. Marta had led us right up to the front door of the Grange House.

When we parked and walked toward the group of people, I noticed Muir relax even more. "These witches are like me," he whispered before we reached them. "They have the magic of the water."

Just as with Marta, Muir seemed to trust these people completely. Me being me, not so much. I realized it was an irrational fear. Just like the night before had been irrational anger. It felt like something outside of me was forcing its way in and competing with my real emotions.

Regardless, I was wary of them, because accepting these people meant I had to accept myself for who and what I was. I hadn't been willing to do that until this moment. Not ever, not even when I was a child and discovered I could manipulate things around me, did I truly believe in my abilities. I spent my life trying to block them from my consciousness. I never wanted to have magic. I simply wanted to be... normal.

After greeting the group outside and being told they were the representatives of the town's Water Guild, they led us inside to meet the leaders of the other guilds, each representing different elements.

Marta told our story and Muir shared details about his journey and how important it had been to find me. Then he talked about how I needed to return with him to the British Isles to complete his quest.

As they talked, I watched people's expressions. Some were rapt with attention, others looked skeptical, and a few sent very obvious looks my way. Maybe they could sense I didn't trust them, or maybe they were wary of outsiders in general, although they didn't seem to mind Muir.

I found that the most interesting since I wasn't a freaking Selkie, but I kept my thoughts to myself and tried to school my expression. When Muir and Marta finished speaking, an elderly man, who looked close to a hundred years old, turned to me. "What are your thoughts about all this, young man?"

"Um," I stammered, taken off guard, before finding my voice. "I think it sucks."

Several people around me chuckled at my honest answer. The elderly man, who was clearly well regarded in the group, shook his head. "I'm not sure you realize just how much this might suck," he responded.

The room fell quiet. "I rarely come to the meetings anymore," he said. "I'll be one hundred and three years old next month, but I am one of the last water seers in Chemeketa. My entire life, I ached for the day a Selkie would come to our shores. And finally, last night, I dreamed the Selkie would come, and he'd bring someone very important to our community."

I looked around the group for confirmation that the old man wasn't some hack making all this up just because of Muir and Marta's story. But the look of awe on the faces around me conveyed he was a venerated man deserving my respect. I noticed a few older people nodding, which could mean he'd shared this with them before.

"The dream has always been vague. Regardless, I always knew the Selkie's arrival would be followed by an oppressive darkness, one that threatened not only him and all Selkie, but our town as well."

I looked at him strangely. "How would Muir's arrival jeopardize you?" I asked.

"I think it's because you may be my brother," said a man who'd sat watching me intensely the entire time we'd been here.

"Our brother," another man said from across the circle we were sitting in.

"Wait? What?" I asked. "I'm from Tennessee. I'm not even from this part of the world."

A middle-aged woman calling herself Donna who'd remained silent throughout the discussion, spoke next, "You three can discuss that later, but for now, know that darkness never travels alone. We can feel the ones Muir describes as Dorcha, and the dark energy that gathers with them is growing. We have to assume the level of intense negativity will continue to increase over time."

The entire room nodded after she finished speaking. "Is my being here putting you all in jeopardy?" Muir asked.

The sense of unease among the group was palpable, before the elderly man spoke again, "Darkness always threatens to overtake the light. Your quest is important, or you wouldn't have attracted this much opposition."

Donna, whom I now assumed was another leader of this community, looked around the room. After getting several nods in acknowledgment, she said, "We will help you, but first, you should speak to the mayor and Crea. And do it soon since we don't have much time. Elizabeth, why don't you take these folks to the diner and feed them, so they all have a place to speak on neutral ground."

She looked at the two men who'd just claimed to be my brothers, and the message was clear even to me. She was warning them not to overwhelm me. *Well, lady*, I thought, *too damned late for that.*

I was ready to bolt, just drive back to my cozy cottage and lock the doors. I wasn't made for all this drama, and I sure as hell didn't want to be in the middle of some ridiculous fake family reunion. *Brothers, seriously?* I turned to tell Marta I was leaving when I saw her smiling from ear to ear at the young woman. "Elizabeth, how is your mom?" she asked.

"Oh, she's as grumpy as ever."

Marta chuckled. "So, is this one of her bad days?"

Elizabeth shook her head. "No, not particularly. She got to the restaurant on time this morning, and I'd already made all the pastries before she arrived so she should be fine."

Marta chuckled as she explained that Amelia, Elizabeth's mother, owned the local restaurant and pastry shop. Everyone knew that the later Amelia arrived at the shop, the grumpier she'd be. I wasn't sure why that was funny. I'd never had much tolerance for anyone who gave lousy service just because they were in a bad mood.

As the women continued chatting, I looked over at the two men who'd made their brash statements of brotherhood and sighed. One was on the phone while the other was butting in on whatever conversation they were having. I groaned, and Muir slipped his hand into mine.

"Do you think these men may truly be your siblings?" he asked.

I shook my head. "No, not possible. I... damn, I wish I hadn't come."

Muir hung his head, and I realized I'd stuck my foot in my mouth. "I'm very sorry for all this, David," Muir said, sounding defeated. I draped my arm around him, forcing myself to let go of the frustration clawing at me.

"You know it's not your fault. This is all just a lot for me to take in right now. Let's go meet them, have some lunch, and see what the... well, see what they want."

The moment we walked into the restaurant, I understood why the community tolerated a grumpy server. Delicious-looking baked goods filled a display case, and the mouthwatering smells coming from the kitchen could make a statue cry.

Elizabeth walked in and yelled out, "Mom, we have special guests."

A middle-aged woman poked her head out of the back, and I could tell she was about to lay into her daughter when she laid eyes on Muir. "Well, bless my soul," she said unsteadily.

She wasted no time walking up to introduce herself. "I'm Muir," he immediately said, and reached out to take the woman's outstretched hand. "It's nice to meet you."

"I'm Amelia," she responded. "Please, let me show you to a table."

The moment we were alone, Marta asked him what the hell that was all about.

Muir chuckled. "Amelia has the sea in her as well. It's distant, but she can still sense who and what I am."

"Really?" Marta looked at him, confused. "I would've never guessed that."

"Really, but I've never met another sea creature before," Amelia said as she came up behind Marta, smiling. She then directed her attention to Muir and placed a plate of fresh sliced salmon and tuna in front of him, although we hadn't ordered yet. "Why are you here?"

"It's a quest," Marta said in a hushed voice before Muir had a chance to answer. "One that should be kept on a need-to-know basis. No offense, Amelia, but it's dangerous."

"I'm guessing that's why all that nasty is gathered along our shores."

We all three nodded, but Marta had a point. We needed to keep word of the quest to ourselves, only informing those who needed to know and could help us.

Muir quickly devoured the food, and I realized we hadn't fed him breakfast earlier. I ordered coffee and one of the pastries, and when it came, I talked Muir into trying a bite. I didn't want to make him sick, but if we ended up making a long cross-country trek to get to the Atlantic, he'd have to eat regular food at some point.

We were just about to finish eating when the two men from the meeting came in, spotted us, and walked over to our table.

"Ugh," I said under my breath. "Here we go."

Marta gently backhanded my chest. "Behave, these are Gwen Franklyn's grandchildren and are very well respected in this town."

I was just about to ask her who Gwen Franklyn was, but it was too late. I suddenly realized there were more of them than I had anticipated. Not two, but three men were walking toward us.

We all stood to greet them, although I'd rather have told them to get lost, but I was feeling generous because of Muir. After the men introduced themselves, Marta gently touched Muir on the shoulder and turned to me.

"I think this conversation is between the four of you. Muir, why don't we take a tour of town and give them some privacy?"

I quickly turned a heated glare on my friend, but damned if she didn't smirk. I leaned over and whispered, "You are in so much trouble."

She chuckled and, after Muir gave me a supportive glance, he took Marta's arm and the two left the restaurant.

I sat back down and stared at the three men in front of me, resisting the strong urge to lash out at them. "May we speak freely?" the one who'd introduced himself as Lance Franklyn, and who served as Chemeketa's mayor, asked.

"Listen, I'm not one for playing games. I don't know why you think I'm your brother or related to you in any way. Like I said, I was born in Tennessee."

"Is this your father?" the one named Kyle asked as he thrust a picture at me.

I almost didn't look at it, the desire to argue nearly overpowering. But one glance at the photo obliterated any argument from me. "Holy shit."

I took the picture and stared at it for a long time. There he was. The man who'd disappeared so long ago. The one I'd secretly come to Oregon to find but had found no trace of him. I'd figured he lied about where he came from, about *everything*, but fuck, here he was. Smiling at the camera as if that one picture hadn't just blown apart everything I thought I knew about my father.

As fast as my shock had come on me, so now did my skepticism. "How did you get this? What kind of scam are you trying to pull?"

Lance chuckled. "We are definitely related. Listen, we aren't pulling a scam. The moment you walked into the Grange House, I felt two things. That you and I were kin, and you're haunted by the same damned curse the three of us have had to fight off. That can only mean you must be the brother we've been looking for."

"I... why... you had a feeling?"

Anger boiled inside me, and I stood to leave. Several other people in the restaurant looked our way, but I didn't give a fuck. I was over this charade. Beyond over it.

I burst out the restaurant and onto the street. I heard footsteps following me, no doubt belonging to one of the brothers, and I turned to yell at them to piss off, only to be met by a... *an actual dragon!*

I heard the restaurant door open again but I was frozen in place. "Kyle, tone it down a little," one of the men said.

With that, the dragon transformed in a blinding flash into the man who'd handed me the picture.

I stood staring, still too damned scared to move. "Did you just turn into a dragon?" I asked, thinking I must be hallucinating.

"Sorry, but you need to listen to us, and I can tell our dad's cantation is manipulating you," he said.

I looked to my left to see another man rushing toward us. He reached us before I had time to respond. "Kyle, you can't turn into a damned dragon in front of everyone in town, shit."

Then he turned to me and said, "Hi, my name is Drew. I'm this one's better half," he said, pointing his thumb at

Lance. "Will you join us at my house before these idiots blow every cover we have?"

Something about him put me at ease, much more than the other guys. I looked around to see if anyone had been surprised by the appearance and disappearance of a huge dragon, but no one seemed to care.

"I'll come, but you do that dragon thing again and I'm out, got it?" I asked, and Kyle blushed and nodded.

I glanced at the three brothers as I followed the men to a farmhouse on a hill not far from the beach. Even though I'd like to throw our whole conversation out a fucking window, I could see we shared a resemblance. Similar features... ones I'd also seen in my father's face.

"Let's sit out in the garden," Drew said.

We followed him to a small sitting area surrounded by what must have been every flower known to humankind. It was lovely, and the smell was heady.

"So," Lance began, "...welcome to the family."

# Fourteen

## Muir

AFTER WE FINISHED EATING, Marta gave me a tour of the village, pointing out small shops that weren't immediately obvious to the regular tourist. Small openings in the sides of buildings, homes, and even stone walls that didn't look like doors were, in fact, entrances to magical shops.

Meeting the water-based witch encouraged me. My inner senses warred between my need to trust these people and my fear of trusting the wrong people.

I had very little choice, and although I could sense the powerful witches around me, I decided to be forthcoming about my quest.

I felt anxious about that choice until I met the woman called Amelia. I hadn't detected the sea in the daughter Elizabeth, but I could sense Amelia and I were related even if I wasn't quite sure how.

There are several cousin creatures in the sea. The Dorcha was, of course, the closest relative of the Selkie, but before the Dorcha had broken away, a tribe of people who hadn't wanted to take on the figure of an animal had become what humans referred to as Mer people.

At one time there had been many different tribes all over the world, but there were very few left since scores had been killed during medieval times. They'd been seen as evil, and human stories were told of the women luring sailors to their death. There might have been some truth to that since sailors of the time were actively killing them.

Ultimately, Mer people escaped to remote places around the globe, and not even the Selkie knew much about them any longer.

Elizabeth found us about an hour after we left the store and told us the community leaders would like to meet with us again that evening.

I didn't know exactly how these people were going to help us, but after spending time in their town, I knew it was a welcoming place, and I could feel they were good people.

I wondered how David was doing. I had so many siblings, I didn't understand why his having only a few caused him such distress. Though my parents were a mated pair, not all Selkie remained monogamous, so it wasn't unusual to have numerous half-siblings. Our community was also relatively small, and young ones were highly regarded. We were all raised by the community as well as our parents, no matter what type of relationship those parents had.

I supposed learning he had siblings when he'd thought himself the only child of either parent must have come as a shock. I hoped he wasn't too upset by the revelation. Their shared features made it obvious the four men were related.

I asked Marta her opinion on David's frame of mind.

She sighed. "He will be okay, Muir, but he's certainly struggling with this information."

"Do you think they really are his brothers?"

She hesitated, then nodded. "Yes, and there is more to it than just meeting family. I was here for a community celebration and saw Lance battle his father's curse first-hand. I almost went to another dimension to help fight the same curse last summer. It's been scary. If David is related to these brothers, then he is facing some serious dark energy."

I thought about that for a moment. "Do you think the quest I'm bringing to David could be jeopardized by his father's curse?"

She shrugged. "I think it's good you found out a curse is on him, especially if you're going to face the dark forces that're chasing you."

I'd need to think about that. It was one thing to bring the Dion Adair to my people. It was another to bring his very real personal demons.

"Are you okay?" Marta asked and I shook my head.

"No, not really," I answered honestly. "There's a lot to consider, for me and the future of my people."

# FIFTEEN

## DAVID

"WHERE IS HE NOW?" I asked, finally accepting that these three men were indeed my brothers.

"He's in a nursing home near Portland," Crea, the middle brother, said.

"We hadn't seen him in years and only found him recently," Kyle, the youngest brother, said. Well, youngest of the three anyway.

"When did you learn about me?" I asked, feeling defensive all of a sudden.

I'd spent my entire life competing with my over-achieving stepsiblings, only to discover I had biological brothers I'd never known about. The revelation left me feeling excited, angry, and cheated, all at the same time. Maybe if I'd known about them, I wouldn't have felt so alone since my mom died.

"When we visited him," Lance said. "He's had a stroke, so he couldn't speak, but we were able to connect with him. He showed us images of you when you were little."

I stood up and paced to the window of the small cozy room. "So, until recently, you didn't know I existed. I still don't get it. Why would you visit him after all this time, especially when he'd cursed you?"

Drew, Lance's partner, went over to the mantel, took down a small wooden box, and handed it to me. "This was left by your grandmother, Gwen. She and I had been roommates, and she entrusted me with four boxes, one to be given to each of her grandsons after she passed. This is the last box, meant for you."

I started to respond, feeling the anger rising, when Drew lifted his hand to stop me. "Before you ask, Gwen only knew that this box was meant for someone connected to her, someone important. She didn't know who you were or that you existed. Your father hadn't told her about you."

"How do you know?" I asked accusingly.

"We considered asking her, but she explained it all in a letter we found," Drew said.

"Asking her? Is she alive? I thought you said she'd passed. I'd like to speak with her."

Drew shook his head. "She died years ago, but she's still with us. If you like, I can summon her, but she's weak now. Please sit down, David, we have a lot to discuss, and if you are going on a quest with a Selkie to protect his people from... well, you should know the stories about your siblings and your birth father."

I did as he asked and listened while Lance explained how our father had cursed them, then how they'd thrown a curse back at him. They spoke frankly about their own lives, of living under that curse, and now in the aftermath of having vanquished it.

They'd experienced one bad relationship after another, before they met their current significant others, the ones who helped them break the curse. The story that resonated with me the most was Kyle's. He'd avoided relationships, then almost destroyed what he was building with his lover, Conley. Who, incidentally, was also a dragon... and from another dimension. Who knew after meeting with and sleeping with a Selkie, I could still be surprised.

"So, what does all this have to do with me?" I asked.

Kyle leaned forward. "Have you ever been in a long-term relationship with another man?" he asked.

I shook my head. "No, but I'm only..."

"I get it," he said, interrupting me. "Before all this went down with me and Conley, I argued that I just didn't want a relationship, but be honest with yourself. Have you dated men and then just lost interest for no apparent reason?"

"And did you ever find the guys you were attracted to, then tried to take advantage of you?" Lance asked.

"Only losers?" Crea added.

I shrugged. "Yeah, but isn't that just part of being gay?"

All three brothers chuckled. "Well, you have that in common, too, plus you show up here? Of all places?" Drew asked.

"I mean, it's a strange coincidence but not that unusual, right?" I asked.

"Here's what we can tell you," Lance said. "All three of us have overcome the curse in our own way. It should be gone, destroyed, yet it remains. Weaker, of course, but it's still there. Grandma left that fourth box for someone. None of us, not even her, were sure why, and then we discovered we have a fourth brother. Now you're here, and you have to admit, it sounds like you're already part of this, like it or not."

I looked down at the box in my hand, feeling almost as if keeping it closed would keep everything they'd said from being true. I didn't want to inherit a curse. I'd wanted family and to find my birth father, but even that was mostly because I felt so betrayed by my stepfather.

"Listen, I don't know what to do with all this. I mean, I'm a solitary person. I-I..." It took me a moment to get my head on straight. "I've wanted a relationship with my dad, and even though I hated him as a kid, I wondered about him as I've gotten older. After my mom died, I tried to find him. When I couldn't, I just gave up. Now you three are here saying we're brothers, and I'm like, where the hell have you been all my life? I need time. I'm going to go because whether you mean it or not, it's a lot to take in. Too fucking much. I'm sorry."

I pushed my chair back and turned to head out the door.

"David, if I may?" Crea said as he also stood up, reaching out to stop me from leaving. "I know this is hard, and yeah, it's too much. But think about it, and if you have questions or want more information, just let us know, okay? We're all committed to helping you through this. You don't have to accept us as family to have our support and help. Okay?"

I looked at him, then at the other men claiming to be my birth family. Brothers or not, they were still complete strangers, and it'd take more than one conversation for me to trust them even under normal circumstances. I nodded at Crea, but didn't say anything and headed out the door and down the street back to find Marta and

Muir. I was ready to be done with all this—the lies, the truth, the people, and this place. Why the hell had I agreed to come to Chemeketa?

# Sixteen

## Muir

WHEN DAVID REJOINED MARTA and me, he appeared frustrated, and I could sense the swirl of emotions raging inside him. I wanted to console him somehow, but he launched into relaying what his newly found brothers had told him.

"Muir, I... apparently, my birth father cast a curse on me and my brothers. They each subdued it in their own way, and now it's on my shoulders to banish the damn thing."

We listened closely as he explained further, telling us of his grandmother's bequeathed stones and his father's whereabouts. Finally, Marta hugged David, and said, "It all makes sense now. It also sounds like your brothers are your best allies for overcoming this curse."

As she released him, she sighed. "The town called a council meeting that's about to start. We need to haul ass to the Grange House."

We were once again seated in a circle with the community leaders, including David's brothers, who sat alongside us. To start the meeting, the old water seer who'd introduced himself as Darrel turned to Lance, and said, "We have debated this very thoroughly, and the Water Guild has decided to help the Selkie the best way we can. Most of us are descended from witches saved during the dark times by Selkie just like Muir." I'd heard stories from our Elders of that history. The first Dion Adair had taught my people to watch for women, possibly witches, who were weighted down and left to drown by angry mobs.

"Because the Selkie helped our ancestors, and we have all witnessed the powers of darkness that plague the Franklyn family, we are willing to take a greater risk for you..." he said, before directing his gaze at David. "...than we normally would."

He drew in a deep breath, then let it out slowly as if what he was about to say was something he feared.

"Learning magic is a lifelong pursuit, David. It isn't something to be gained quickly, and much if not most of that is because a practitioner must know and respect the consequences of using it. I'm sure that had your grandmother, Gwen, known you existed, she would've reached out to you and brought you here to Chemeketa to at least learn the basics of our craft, much like she did with your brothers. Instead, like them, you have avoided your gifts and pushed them away. That concerns us, because we've learned over the years that those who scorn their gifts often scorn all magic. That being said, the Selkie are in danger and we all must do what we can to help."

Darrel then turned to Marta. "Can you vouch for David's character?" he asked. "Even to the point that it may impact or cost the lives of others?"

Marta looked pained for a moment as she studied David. "Yes," she finally responded, "I would trust David with my life."

"Then you shall," Darrel said. "David, because the journey you are taking is outside our influence, we can't help you directly, like we have your brothers. We understand the curse that even in its weakened state still plagues you. We also understand you will be on your own, in the middle of great oceans. The Water Guild has decided to grant you use of our combined knowledge of the element of water."

He paused then, looking around the circle. Several heads nodded in agreement, and I suspected the leaders had been negotiating these details since our first meeting had ended this morning. In giving their magic, they were in essence giving themselves, and I wondered if David realized the magnitude of what they were offering him and, by extension, me.

"Others on this council may choose to lend you their knowledge as well. If you accept this offer, you will inherently know how to use magic to protect yourself, how to create and destroy, and all that our powers entail. Be warned, however, anything you do with our knowledge will come back on us as well as you. If you misuse our gift, you will be putting our lives at risk. Do you understand?"

David looked sick. "I don't want this," he said reluctantly, as if to himself.

Marta put her hand over his. "David, it's very powerful and maybe even scary, what they are offering. But so is the darkness we can all feel surrounding us. We have to assume this is incredibly important. You should accept their gift."

David stared at the floor as the room of people quietly waited for his response. When he finally looked up at Darrel, he asked, "What's the catch?"

The old man nodded. "Of course, you are wise to know there would be one. You must return when the quest is over, so we can retract the spell, then you must promise to live among us for no less than one year as we train you in using your gifts and all that you have learned in a responsible way."

"Will I be able to leave, or will I have to stay here the entire year?"

Several of the attendees chuckled at his question. "You won't be a prisoner in our town," Darrel said, and shook his head. "But you must live here and learn, and willingly commit to both."

David nodded and looked at me. After holding his breath, he let it out slowly, before asking, "You are sure, Muir, that I'm the one who has to do this?"

I nodded. "The Dion Adair's stone brought me to you, and now the Dorcha are strengthening their forces, because they know you are the one who can help us. Yes, I'm sure."

David returned his attention to Darrel, and asked, "Will I be able to lead a normal life once this is over?"

Several people in the group looked skeptical while others shook their heads, but Donna, who'd spoken last time we were here, responded, "If by normal, you mean a life devoid of magic, that all depends on you. Once you are given access to all that we know and have learned over years of practice, you will be a very powerful witch.

You can't unlearn what you will acquire from this spell. However, you can choose to do with it as you wish. But be assured, just as you've grown and changed from experiences throughout life, you won't remain the same person you were before."

David nodded, then looked me in the eyes, as he said, "I will accept the offer."

I knew this decision was difficult for David, and one he wasn't making lightly. He treasured his life of solitude. Even though I liked my solitude as much as anyone, I preferred the company of my people, of my family, I could understand how much he was giving up by taking this on. Where any number of humans and witches alike would've jumped at the chance, I could see David would've preferred never to have had this thrust on him.

I hated that it was me taking away the simplicity of the life he treasured so much. One man's sacrifice might be a small price to pay for the safety of an entire civilization, but that man was someone I was beginning to deeply care about. Regardless of his greater purpose, I already knew that given the choice, I would willingly sacrifice myself to ensure his safety.

"Then, we will begin at once," Darrel said. "If the dark ones continue gathering in greater numbers, we won't be able to control them by nightfall."

The spell they cast seemed simple. Everyone remained in the room, including me. I was surprised at being allowed to stay, but Darrel had said knowledge of the ways of the Selkie might be the most important skill David acquired.

The spell only took a short time to cast. The group placed David in the middle of the room and surrounded him. Darrel and a woman whose name I hadn't learned poured salt around the outside of the building, then returned and chanted a few lines in a language I didn't recognize.

The rest of the group began to chant along with them, and I found even I was able to chant the phrases, their pronunciation and meaning becoming clearer to me as the spell wore on.

*"Ohtha, Brathe, Omat, Quey…"*

All that's within us shall be in you.

*"Ronda, Frotha, Emetta Fray…"*

Knowledge of power, magic, and truth.

*"Estwa, Forma, Entrese, Amund."*

Combine within you and bears its fruit.

We chanted as the air in the room became heavy. It began to feel as if the top of my skull was being lifted off, and I could actually see a fog-like substance rising from the other participants that flowed over David before absorbing into him.

As the spell continued, David went into a trance and his mouth began to work the spell with us, although I knew by looking at him he was no longer conscious.

As the spell drew to a close, we all chanted a final phrase.

*"With harm to none, so mote it be."*

Almost as if someone had slammed a door shut, the lingering fog in the room rushed into David and sealed itself within him. David remained unconscious, but standing.

Darrel looked pale, as did several others in the room. Clearly, the casting had taken more of a toll on the older participants than those of us who were younger.

"You must leave now before the sun sets. The powers of darkness have already crossed a threshold beyond our abilities to defend against it, at least for long. And there is no time to draw in others from our outlying areas."

I nodded and asked how we were going to leave.

"I will take you," a young man, much younger than me, said. "I'm a pilot and can fly you inland, away from the sea's dark creatures."

"Fly?" I asked, and immediately began to panic.

"You'll be fine," Marta said before addressing the young man. "Is there room for me to fly with you? I can help comfort Muir since this will be overwhelming for him."

"We'll need room for us as well," Lance asked, waving between himself and his brothers. "We still need to speak with David, and can do so during the flight."

The young man nodded, then said, "My plane has room, and don't worry, Selkie, it will only take us a night to get you to the other side of the country. The dark ones won't be able to track you in the air. That's what we all believe to be the case, at least."

Despite the knot in my stomach, I nodded. No, the Dorcha had no access to the land or air, so as long as the curse that plagued David didn't communicate our movements, as the people of this town feared, they wouldn't be able to trace me. "Okay, let's fly."

# Seventeen

## David

I WOKE UP TO the sound of an airplane engine. When I opened my eyes, it was worse than I'd imagined. We were in one of those private jets that were way too small for my comfort, although this one was beautifully decorated with a clean white-leather interior. My newly found brothers were sitting in chairs facing Marta and Muir.

Marta noticed me and winked, but she was busy chanting something at Muir, who looked like he might puke, pass out, or both.

"I see I'm not the only one not cut out for flying," I said, teasing him.

His eyes were wide and glassy, and I could tell Marta's chanting was to calm him, although it clearly wasn't working very well. Or, maybe it was, and he'd be even worse off without her right now.

I was sitting across the small plane from them, so I got up and sat on the other side of Muir. When I pulled him into my side, I felt his pelt between us. I placed it on his lap, and he immediately let out a sigh and snuggled into me. "This is so scary," he whispered.

"Freaks me out too," I admitted.

Marta continued to chant next to us, but holding each other helped more than anything.

"We wanted to give you time to ask questions," Lance said. "I know it's a rush, but we didn't want you to go without being able to speak with us."

"You should also probably open the box," Crea said, holding up the small wooden box our grandmother had left me. He must have pocketed it after I'd left it behind when I bolted from the farmhouse.

I didn't respond as he placed the box in my hand. Accepting the inevitable now, I did as he suggested. A shimmering bracelet was nestled inside, woven with mother of pearl and shells commonly found along our part of the Oregon coast. A bright blue sapphire shone from the middle of a small shell, where you'd expect to see a pearl in an oyster. It was lovely.

The bracelet seemed to radiate energy. I slipped it over my wrist, unable to take my eyes off it.

"We never summoned our grandmother, but after we land, we should. You need to know who she is, because now that you have that," Lance said as he pointed at the bracelet, "I'm sure you will have access to her. That could be very important."

I nodded, immediately feeling more at ease with the bracelet on my wrist. "I have questions about our dad. Do you mind if I ask about him?" I asked the men who sat across from me. *My brothers.* That was going to take some getting used to.

All three looked at me expectantly. "We haven't been close for years, but we'll tell you what we can," Crea said.

We talked most of the way across the continent, my brothers sharing their good memories of our father as well as the bad, and how he'd once been a devout witch before turning his back on magic. They also told me more about our grandma, Gwen, and I felt more of a loss for never having known her than all the lonely years I'd spent wondering about my birth father.

I continued listening until my mind felt like it could explode from information overload, then said, "When I return, I'll have to stay in Chemeketa for a year. That's what I agreed to, so maybe we can get to know each other better then."

That seemed to mollify my brothers, although it was still hard to think of them as that. Muir and I ended up dozing off as Marta continued chanting. I had to guess her chants were helping us both.

We woke up a few hours later as we were landing.

"Just in time," Marta said. The woman looked utterly exhausted. "We're making our final descent. I'm sorry I couldn't hold the chant any longer. I wanted to get you on the ground before you woke up."

"You look like you've done all you can," I said, concerned to see my friend so tired.

She reached over Muir and took my hand.

"Hold on, this will be a bumpy landing," our pilot said.

I immediately felt my stomach roll as we hit turbulence and the plane bumped in the sky. When I saw Muir panicking, it was almost like someone had turned on a water spigot in my brain. I immediately knew how to calm the air around us.

*"Soft air flows, for magic knows, ease the ride to land this load."*

I felt the plane steady, and the pilot yelled back, "Wow, that's some powerful magic, thanks. Only my grandmother can ease a plane's descent like that."

*She must've been at the council meeting last night*, I thought.

When we finally landed, I could feel the relief flowing off Muir. Then I turned my attention to my fatigued friend. "Marta, I'm going to help you out, okay?"

When she didn't resist, I knew she'd really overdone it, because Marta wasn't one to accept help without complaining a little first.

As with the turbulence, I knew instinctively how to draw energy to her. "Lance, Crea, Kyle, I need to loan Marta energy, but I need to draw from you. Do you mind?" I asked, wondering why the men hadn't already offered that to her... or for her to ask for it herself. I had to assume it was because everyone was so preoccupied they didn't think of it, and Marta was probably too busy trying to keep Muir from freaking out.

When they all nodded their agreement, I began forming the spell in my mind. Marta's energy mostly came from the earth, which explained why she wasn't well grounded as we flew across the night sky. She'd done the very thing she'd warned me against and used her own energy instead of pulling from her source.

I didn't have to chant. Mostly, I was able to borrow from my brothers as well as myself. Still, Crea's energy was the strongest, and I assumed that was because he shared the same energy as Marta.

As energy flowed from us into her, Marta's color returned to normal, and she yawned. "That's amazing," she said as we all stood up. "I'm not going to get off the plane.

I feel so sleepy that I'll say my goodbyes here. Muir, it was a pleasure to meet you. I wish you great luck on your quest."

She turned to me and took my hand. "My friend," she said. "I'm afraid for you. I know you're endowed with the knowledge of the townspeople, but don't take unnecessary risks. Even with the power you've been granted, there's much you don't understand."

She then took Muir's hand. "Please, take care of each other."

I embraced her and didn't try to stop the tears as they flowed. Marta was my one true friend on this planet. She'd stuck by me through our years together and had been both a mentor and companion. I feared what was ahead of us, but mostly I feared facing the unknown without her.

The rest of us headed to the home of one of the pilot's friends, who was out of town. On the drive there, I called my boss at the whale-watching tour company to say I'd likely be out for the season, if not two, due to a family emergency, which was at least somewhat truthful. She wasn't thrilled, but sounded understanding. My marine biology work was all research-based, so no one would likely even notice my absence for a long while. Still, I set an out-of-office email stating I'd taken a sabbatical to study sea life in Scotland, which also wasn't exactly true, but close enough that I didn't feel like a liar.

As soon as we arrived at the house, my brothers convinced me it was time I meet our grandmother, Gwen. After the draining day we'd had, I'd much rather have just turned in for the night. But considering I might never get the chance again if things went to shit on this quest,

I couldn't pass up the opportunity to meet my grandma. It turned out the ceremony wasn't that intense. The four of us joined hands while Muir sat behind us. My brothers simply clasped hands and closed their eyes to summon her and literally like... well, magic, she appeared.

The moment she saw me, tears sprang to her eyes. I couldn't actually hear her speaking, but her voice came through loud and clear in my mind. "Drew told me your brothers had found you, David. I'm so sorry I didn't know about you."

I didn't know what else to do but shrug and try to offer some reassurance. "You can't help what you didn't know, but at least I'm getting to meet you and getting to know these guys," I said, no longer feeling the anger I'd initially felt.

I looked down at the bracelet on my wrist and could sense it was somehow blocking the negative energy that had plagued me most of my life. That in and of itself was overwhelming and proof that I'd been as manipulated by a family curse I hadn't even known about.

"You are going on a very intense journey, so let me say this. The darkness that was your father's curse will seek to prevent you from succeeding on this quest. I'll be with you as much as I can. Hold onto that bracelet. That's your connection to me. If, for any reason, you feel you need my help, close your eyes, and summon me just like the boys did, okay?" she asked.

I could tell she was getting weaker from the conversation, so I didn't ask any questions. I just nodded. It wasn't like I knew what to ask anyway. I was exhausted, physically, mentally, and emotionally, even spiritually, if I was honest. I just wanted to find a bed and crash and hope that somehow everything would seem better in the morning.

Then, just as suddenly as she'd appeared, she vanished. "We need to get back to the plane. The pilot is holding his plane for us," Lance said. "He has already cleared it with his friend for you to stay here tomorrow too, but I can feel you need to move on as soon as possible. The head start you've been given still doesn't buy you much time."

I nodded, then shook the three men's hands as I walked them outside. I might have accepted them as my brothers, but we weren't at the hugging stage yet. "Oh, and take care of Marta for me," I said, thinking how lame that must sound. She was a powerful witch, but she was also vulnerable and worried about me and Muir.

The three guys smiled at me and agreed to continue sending her energy as they flew back to Oregon. That was the least I could hope for. When they left, I dragged myself back into the house, determined to get a few more hours of sleep before continuing on our journey.

# Eighteen

## Muir

According to David, we'd been dropped off inland. "This should keep the Dorcha from noticing you," he'd said.

I figured it was true, but the Dorcha occupied all the world's oceans. As soon as I came in contact with the water, I'd be vulnerable. At least I knew the Atlantic better than I did the Pacific. I could avoid them much more if I were in my own familiar waters.

"How will you get to where we're going?" I asked David shortly after landing.

"Simple, we'll fly to Scotland."

Clearly, David expected us to continue our journey side by side. I had no desire to go back up in one of those flying machines, but sailing on the human ships would just put us at risk. The Dorcha had already threatened us and that was on land, albeit over a waterway. I had no desire to see how they might try to impede us in the water.

"I'd like one more night with you, alone, before that journey," I told him, and he graciously agreed.

I'd felt the Dorcha before as I swam through the oceans between Scotland and David's home. Selkie rarely left our part of the world, our homeland waters, so I'd figured even sea creatures who knew what I was didn't care much about me passing through.

It was the Dion Adair's stone I had carried on me that alerted the Dorcha to my presence. Our sharing Selkie ancestors enabled them to follow the stone's direction, in much the same way it served to guide me. Because of that, they also now knew who David was to us, which put him in even greater danger than simply traveling with me. I had no doubt they considered my journey out of our homeland to be an invasion and thus in violation of the agreement my ancestors had made with the Dorcha so long ago.

They would be searching for me and the stone. They would be searching for David.

I shivered as David sat next to me, pulling me into his side. As a human, the chill in the air bothered me more than when I had my pelt on. Just thinking of the pelt, I reached over and pulled it closer, wanting to feel the comfort it gave me. It wasn't the cold that made me shiver, though. It was the fear of what we would face when we arrived in Scotland.

David must've noticed my discomfort, because he stood up and took me with him, leading me to the guest bedroom. He took charge this time, gently draping my pelt over the back of a chair before completely undressing me. As his hands slid up and down my naked form, my mind shifted from fear to lust for the man-witch I'd started to develop feelings for. I was sure this wasn't how things were supposed to go. I'd only found him to fulfill a quest, my destiny, to save my people. I should be neutral when it came to David. I should be...

All thoughts slipped out of my head as David pushed me onto the bed and slid down my body before taking me into his mouth.

I moved between his parted lips luxuriously, enjoying the feel of his mouth's warmth around my cock. When he pulled back, I rolled over, giving him access to my backside, and he immediately moved behind me and slid his cock up and down my arse.

I moaned as what tension I still had left melted out of my body. "I want you," I admitted to him. "I want you inside me."

David all but growled, causing me to chuckle. "Will you take me, David?" I asked and he nodded into my neck, kissing the soft skin just below my ear.

He pulled away then and I wanted to cry from the loss of feeling his body against mine, but he returned a moment later. He opened a package, and poured something slick down my arse crack. "W-wow... what is that?" I asked, looking back at him surprised.

David smiled. "Lube. It makes this easier."

Then he began to slip his finger into me, and I decided I had an affinity for this *lube*, as he called it. I moaned as he stretched my arsehole with one finger, then added another. Before long, I was a loose piece of seaweed ready to be manipulated by the waves.

"I've been tested, I don't have any diseases... but I can use a condom," David said.

I looked at him strangely. "What's a condom?"

David just smiled, as he often did when I didn't readily comprehend something he'd said. "It... well, it's like a shield. Something to protect against diseases spread by one person to another."

"I understand, but you said you don't have any diseases..." I responded and David pulled my face around gently and kissed me.

"So, you don't mind if we just do this without a condom?"

I shook my head, but I was becoming frustrated that our mating had taken a turn and we were discussing things instead of letting me feel his cock inside my body.

"Just take me, David. I want you inside me."

That was all David needed to hear. He settled his body back behind mine and I soon felt his cock slide up and down my entrance again. This time, because of the slick he'd added, his cock caught on my hole, causing me to suck in air.

"Oh, that's it... yes, David, yes..."

My uncontrollable moaning spurred him on and within moments, he pushed himself inside of me.

Little dots of light sparkled into my vision as my body accepted and adjusted to him. "I... I've never felt anything like this," I croaked, and David paused.

"Are you okay?" he asked, leaning over my back, and whispering in my ear.

"Mmm," I hummed. "I'm so much better than okay. Don't stop, please. I need you, David."

He nuzzled my neck again, then slid his cock the rest of the way in. The stinging quickly subsided, the feeling replaced with one of sheer ecstasy.

David moved inside me while holding me close, my back pressed to his chest. Love poured out of him, and into me, with every stroke. I'd never experienced such emotions with an intimate partner. Perhaps it was too soon, and a relationship would be fraught with challenges, but I also knew better than to question destiny. If the Fates wanted me to love this man, they had certainly started the process. For the moment, though, I just wanted to revel in the feeling of him.

When I began to move against him, trying to impale myself on his cock, he pulled out of me, helped me get on all fours, and glided back into my body—the slow movements from before transformed into more rapid, demanding thrusts.

As good as he'd felt before, nothing compared to how it felt to have David taking me aggressively from behind. I felt owned, wanted, used in the most wonderful way.

Our mating dragged on, each thrust causing my heart to attach itself to him that much more.

Finally, my climax was too close to stave off any longer. I pushed back into David's thrusts, causing him to shift, the little lights sparkling in my vision when he hit my electric spot, as we called it. I yelled as I released and felt David come in me seconds later.

We both collapsed on the bed. Without pulling himself out, David wrapped his arms around me and drew me close, his chest pressed firmly against my back.

"That was amazing," he said, and kissed my neck.

Too many emotions swirled though me at that moment. I had been claimed by the Dion Adair. No matter how things turned out, I knew from this point forward I would belong only to him. Instinctively, I knew that was more information than he could handle.

Selkie mated with whomever they chose whenever they chose, until they were claimed by a lover. It didn't happen for all Selkie, but when it did, they were mated for life. I almost cried as he held me from behind.

When David eventually pulled away, lost to sleep, I whispered, "I love you, Dion Adair. I will be yours forever."

# Nineteen

## David

Using the new knowledge and power given to me by the people of Chemeketa was a strange adjustment. One minute, I'd be thinking like normal, and the next, I'd instinctively know about or how to do something I'd never encountered before.

For example, when we arrived at the airport and Muir saw the private jet we were taking to Scotland, he freaked out. As I felt his anxiety spike, Marta's knowledge of how to calm him immediately sprang to my mind. Not only that, but I also knew what the consequences of using the magic were, so I didn't just react in the moment.

Instead, I reached out, pulling energy from the water in the earth and allowing it to pass through me into Muir. I could feel him relax almost immediately.

As we boarded the plane, he appeared to be in a trance. Once I had Muir tucked into his seat, he dozed off. I began to feel the familiar tug of energy draining from me and let my mind search for anything I could use for grounding, thinking maybe the water aboard the plane might help.

In that moment, another bit of information came to me, but I didn't know the woman who'd gifted it. I could see her in my mind's eye, though. Old and quite frail. She hadn't spoken to us while we'd been in Chemeketa.

She'd been a flight attendant in her youth, and, being a water elemental like me and Muir, she'd learned you could pull energy from the clouds. She'd prided herself in doing that to deal with rowdy or handsy passengers. She'd also used it on occasion to put them to sleep, although she'd always felt guilty about that.

I allowed the cloud energy to flow through me, surprised at its intensity. Doing so gave me pause, since clouds could hold massive amounts of water and energy.

That made me think of hurricanes, so I double-checked the woman's knowledge to make sure I wouldn't inadvertently cause one. Once I was confident it was going to be okay, I lay back and enjoyed the feeling of such immense power flowing through me into Muir.

I turned to him and couldn't help my heart fluttering at the sight of the beautiful man sleeping peacefully next to me.

I'd finally come to accept my part of Muir's journey, and was no longer trying to push him out of my life. I was guessing that was why I saw him differently now. Not as some burden, but a truly miraculous creature. Thinking of the moon that'd appeared to me in the dream by my lagoon, I smiled. *Thank you, goddess.*

Of course, the bracelet hanging off my wrist was likely helping too. I wasn't afraid of getting close to Muir any longer. I wasn't plagued with all his faults, imaginary or real. That shit had been from my birth father's curse. All this time, all the men I'd wanted to like, to date... *Fuck*!

I thought to myself and felt the energy flowing from me to Muir waver.

I refocused, pushing the whirl of emotions regarding my birth father out of my head.

My stepdad had been a good man. I could see that clearly now. Yes, we had our differences. His son and daughter had made life hard on me, although, I thought now, the curse my birth father thrust on me must've also had some impact there. I'd begun thinking better of my stepfamily recently, and had to believe my brothers overcoming the curse had lessened its damaging influence.

Maybe they had never been the problem, maybe it had always been me. Well, not me exactly, but my homophobic birth father. A man I didn't even know, and now didn't care to know, turned out to be at the root of all my problems. I still had to take responsibility for how my life had played out thus far, though, and I wasn't satisfied with much of it. I'd made so many mistakes in relationships and with those who had cared about me.

I looked back at Muir, willing myself to let all that go. Everything I'd learned from the people in Chemeketa told me those negative thoughts would just bring my birth father's darkness to me. I needed to stay focused on the positive, at least while I was on this quest to keep Muir and his people safe.

Muir and I had bonded quickly and were well-matched sexually, both of which would've scared me before. Muir was my perfect man, if I had to choose. When we had sex last night, we'd connected on a deeper, more intense level. I could tell it'd impacted Muir the same way.

Of course, leave it to me that my perfect man was a magical sea creature. I chuckled, noticing Muir smile and realizing my thoughts must be mixed with his. With the link I was holding between us, it stood to reason he would have some connection to my ponderings. Regardless, I didn't try to hide my feelings... I'd begun falling for him.

I began to think about his small, fit body tucked so nicely into mine as we slept. I began gently caressing him, and Muir moaned slightly in his sleep.

*Well, why not enjoy myself,* I figured. We were the only passengers on the plane. The pilot had greeted us when we boarded and said there would be no flight attendant since this was a spur-of-the-moment flight.

Someone in Chemeketa had pulled strings to make it happen. Since Muir and I were alone, I closed my eyes and let my mind drift to how much I loved making love to him.

I used my imagination to picture myself running my hands over his svelte body, and I could sense Muir respond immediately to my touch. Yeah, magic definitely had its advantages.

I must've fallen asleep, because when I opened my eyes, the pilot had marked our route as halfway.

I yawned and stretched, then glanced over and noticed Muir looking at me.

I smiled at him. "You're looking better."

He nodded, a satisfied smirk on his face. "Our mating helped."

I blushed. I didn't honestly think he'd remember. "Yeah, it helped me too."

"I like this new power of yours. I think we should use it again."

I leaned over and kissed him. "They have a bed. Should we use it?"

Just then, turbulence hit, and Muir's panic returned. "Hold on," I said, and immediately pumped up the power. We must've been flying through a storm, because the energy was more aggressive than before. As soon as I connected the energy to Muir, though, he put his hand up to stop me.

"No, I'd rather stay alert," he said. "But thank you, David."

I nodded and leaned over to kiss him again. "I need to stretch my legs. But I understand if you prefer sitting."

"No, as long as the air bouncing isn't too strong, I will be fine."

We began to stand up when the plane dropped several feet and rose again, causing my stomach to do a few loops.

"Or I might just stay here," he said.

I chuckled as I walked around the plane a few times, then bent over into a stretch. When I'd traveled to Europe before, I'd had to sit in uncomfortable seats for hours on end. This flight was a significantly better experience, but still a long haul on a cramped airplane.

Muir watched me as I did my routine and when I stood back up after my stretch, he smiled coyly. "Have you ever, um, been the taker?" he asked.

It took me a moment to realize what he was talking about. "Oh." I chuckled. "You mean, have I ever been a bottom?" He thought for a moment and then nodded.

"I have, but I'm not usually comfortable enough with anyone to do that."

"Would you be comfortable enough with me to try?" he asked.

I thought for a moment. If I could distract him with magic sleep sex, that might be the best option. *Yeah*, I thought once again. This magic stuff wasn't all that bad, really not that bad at all!

# Twenty

## Muir

THE FLYING MACHINE THAT took us to Scotland landed not far from the town of Wick. From there we were able to get a ride to the ferry that crossed over to Orkney. It felt calming, almost reassuring, to be so near open water once again.

My people had abandoned Orkney when it became too populated, and we now lived along the lesser-known islands to the north of the archipelago. But I had spent my *coisich mun cuairth* in this area, as do most Selkie, so I knew it well. Just being this close to home filled a void inside me, like I was back where I belonged.

It was a nice change for me to be showing David around. I planned to safely secure him in one of the tourist cottages and then report to the Council of Elders. If they refused to transform into human form to meet him here on land, we would have to make other arrangements.

I hoped David would be able to fix the barriers, as the Elders expected. Could he ensure our safety as we swam in these waters? Were his powers strong enough to restore the health of our habitat? Could he bring the fish back? The questions were too many, and they weighed heavily on my mind as we rode to the ferry terminal.

The moment the ferry left the dock, I could sense danger around us. I'd never detected Dorcha in our waters, since they had been driven off long before I was born., but they were definitely here now.

The presence of our warriors was strong as well, though not combative. Unfortunately, Having temporarily lost the Dion Adair's stone when I was attacked likely resulted in a standoff between the two factions, which explained the tension I was currently feeling.

David must have felt the Dorcha, too, because without speaking, he placed his arm around me and drew me closer as the ferry sailed toward the Orkneys.

My concern about the Elders proved unfounded. They met us in human form as we disembarked the ferry. David looked strangely at my people, who didn't speak, but turned almost as one and led the way toward a private beach often frequented by seals.

It was clear they were angry. And not just because this was the first time most of these men and women had been out of their pelts since they were my age or younger. I had expected Regani, at least, might offer a welcoming greeting, but she also appeared quite concerned.

When we reached the shore, the seals parted and allowed us to sit amongst them. Our seal counterparts were always much more accepting of us than our human sides were.

"What has happened?" Regani asked, directing the question to me.

I explained how I had journeyed to an entirely different ocean, following the direction the Dion Adair's stone led me. I then recounted being attacked by Dorcha, and how David had rescued me. That I'd lost the stone in the assault, and it hadn't returned to me until David's friend found it following another near-attack.

The Elders listened attentively to my story. Finally, Regani sighed and, taking her mate's hand, said, "I told you it wasn't as they told us."

"*They* who? Told you what?" I asked.

"The Dorcha. Their representatives informed the council that they allowed you to pass through their waters unmolested despite not having sought permission to swim there, and that you attacked one of them unprovoked. They also said your witch man..." she said before glancing over at David, then back at me, "...needlessly attacked their leader and tossed him into the water like unwanted seaweed."

David grunted at the accusation, but otherwise sat silently beside me.

I reached for the sapphire that hung around my neck and handed it to Regani. "Look into the stone. You can see David is our Dion Adair. After the Dorcha took it in the attack, they must've seen it too. It would've revealed to them who David is to our people as well. But I'm curious, why would the Dorcha care about him?"

"We're not sure about that either," Regani admitted. "We needed to hear from you before we spoke with them again. We will meet with their representatives tonight, but we can only guess they will be angry when we confront them with the truth as you have told us."

Caelan, Regani's mate and the leader of our warriors in my absence, took a deep breath before adding, "They are gathering their forces around our borders. You must've felt their warriors as you crossed from the mainland to here. We must prepare for war." That seemed to be all anyone wanted to say, and he turned away, with Regani and the rest of the Elders following, and headed for the sea.

The quickly fading light allowed them to discard their land coverings, as we called clothes, and slip into the water in their seal form unnoticed, but it was a jolt for me to see them change out in the relative open like that. Usually, our people were wary of changing even in waning daylight, let alone so freely amongst other Selkie, but things were different now. We were preparing for war.

"David, I'm sorry. I will have to follow them and see what more I can learn. They'll want to meet with you again to know if you're prepared to fight for us like your ancestor did." He nodded, appearing resolute, but didn't say anything. "Can you find your way back to your shelter on your own, or would you like me to accompany you?"

"No," he said, sounding concerned. "You should go with your people. I'll be fine on my own. But, Muir—" He grasped both my hands before looking me in the eye. "—be careful. The Dorcha almost killed you before. They're dangerous." He blushed and looked out at the sea, where I could now see the Elders swimming in the surf toward our homeland. "I know you know that. I'm just concerned about you."

I kissed David hard on the lips before I pulled away. "You are our Dion Adair, but you know you are also very special to me. I will stay safe and will return to you."

Parting was like having my soul ripped from me. We had to face the challenges as they arose, and that meant I would have to rejoin my people as the warrior I was trained to be, even if it also meant no longer being in David's loving arms.

# TWENTY-ONE

## DAVID

AFTER WATCHING MUIR AND the Elders swim until they disappeared under the waves, a group of people showed up and scooped up the discarded clothing before disappearing up into the darkening night. I immediately set on back toward a bus stop I'd seen on our way to the private beach. Muir had planned to find me accommodations, but I'd already booked a place earlier using the plane's Wi-Fi, and a good thing too, seeing as the Elders had preempted his efforts.

Since I wasn't able to actually join the Selkie in the water, at least I didn't think I could at this point, I wanted to be as near to them as possible. So, I'd chosen a small and secluded seaside cottage. Not that I could really afford it, but I'd save those worries for later.

As I walked along the trail back to the road, I felt rather than saw the Dorcha watching me. They were close. No wonder the Selkie were so antsy. Muir said the Dorcha hadn't occupied this area for over a century, maybe two or three, but they were certainly here now.

The bracelet felt warm on my wrist, and I had to assume it was warning me of danger. Whether the Dorcha were motivated by their hatred of humans, rivalry with the Selkie, or the darkness around my birth father's curse, I couldn't be sure. Regardless, I knew to keep my guard up.

Before reaching the other tourists, I glanced back over the water, and even though it was dark, I thought I saw the outline of a man on the back of a horse. I had no sooner seen it than the voice of one of Chemeketa's leaders filled my head. A former college professor, someone who had studied the myths of the old and new worlds, whispered, "Nuckelavee."

With that, the man's years of scholarly research and knowledge surged through my mind. According to local legend, the Nuckelavee was an evil creature who despised and plagued humans, a powerful being with no natural predators that could wreak havoc with little fear of repercussions. The locals believed that had it not been for its fear of rain and fresh water, it would have driven humanity from the island.

What alarmed me most was if there was any truth to the legend, the monster could live on both land and sea. I increased my pace to the bus stop, where I found other tourists waiting. I doubted the Nuckelavee could've cared less about the tourists or me, but I'd still prefer to be with others if the monster attacked. The level of intense hate radiating offshore, where it and the vicious Dorcha lay in wait, was enough to make me feel ill.

Fortunately, the bus came shortly after I arrived at the stop, and I felt more at ease when the doors closed. I missed Muir. He'd have known more about this creature and how to best defend against it, if not defeat it. That was only part of it, though, I admitted to myself. When

Muir was around, I felt stronger. Like he somehow filled me with additional strength I didn't possess alone. Together, we were powerful.

Again, I rubbed the bracelet, which felt connected to him, although that was absurd. Us both wearing blue sapphires—my grandmother's bracelet, and the Dion Adair's stone he still wore—hadn't gone unnoticed by me, but surely it was a stretch to think everything could be so interrelated. Somehow my birth father's ancestry and my mom's heritage combined into me being the Selkie savior? For real, it was so out there.

The bus stopped half a block from the cottage I'd rented, and when I found the key in the hidey-hole left by the owner, I quickly went in and locked the door behind me.

The professor's thoughts returned, and I grabbed all the bowls and pots I could find and filled them with fresh water from the tap, then put them in front of all the windows and exterior doors.

I knew I was being ridiculous, but if the creature was afraid of fresh water, it was the only line of defense I had if it decided to attack.

That night I slept a couple of hours at most, filled with nightmares of not only the Nuckelavee, but similarly terrifying sea creatures. Fanged serpents lurking in the murky depths that could strike like a snake, and long-necked beasts that resembled the Loch Ness monster. Most didn't have names, but occasionally the professor's thoughts would identify them.

When I woke up for the umpteenth time, sweat pouring off me, I thought, *Finfolk*. The name of the Dorcha in this part of Scotland was Finfolk. They'd plagued not only the Selkie but also humans.

I knew from the professor's memories that the Finfolk had been known by the Vikings, but since then, they'd disappeared from the islands. That gave me some idea of how long the Selkie had lived on these islands alone. It also blew my mind realizing all of the mythical creatures of the deep, frightening or otherwise, had most likely existed, and many may have been the shapeshifting Dorcha.

I opened my phone, thanking the universe I had coverage in this remote area, and began looking for stories of sea monster attacks in recent centuries, but found very little. All the most recent sightings were in the northern waters, and few, if any, involved attacks.

It only went to show that as humans became more sophisticated with their weaponry, these creatures, the Finfolk, or Dorcha, were becoming more concerned about human retaliation. There were a few odd incidents, though, like the recent events of Atlantic orca suddenly attacking sailboats when they'd never done so before. Scientists were baffled, but I figured it was the Dorcha showing their dominance.

Muir had said the Dorcha could shift into any sea creature they wanted. My guess was they were shifting into regular sea life to escape notice by the humans they hated so much.

I finally turned off my phone and plugged it in to charge. After casting a protective shield around the cottage, thanks to Mrs. Ruth, Chemeketa's local pharmacist, I fell into a light sleep.

I thought of Muir, and in my mind's eye I could see him in his seal form, swimming among his people, all of whom appeared alarmed. At one point, he stopped and turned toward me, and I knew he could sense me and was acknowledging my presence.

For one brief and insane moment, I wished I could turn myself into a seal and go swimming in the surf with him and the other Selkie. Then I felt the full force of the darkness the Dorcha launched at them, and it became obvious I wasn't a warrior, or even a potential one.

I preferred peace, strove for it. I had cousins who'd gone into the armed forces after high school, and had tried to get me to enlist, but I'd known then, like I knew now, I wasn't cut out for that life. I avoided conflict of all types rather than ran toward it. Well, until now.

Not that I would ever be able to be a Selkie anyway. Even with the vast knowledge given to me by Chemeketa's leaders, nowhere in that knowledge or skill level was the ability to shapeshift. For now, and the foreseeable future, my place in all of this remained firmly on land.

# Twenty-Two

## Muir

T HE ENTIRE COMMUNITY WAS pulling together. The young and the old were moving into our most secure caves, protected by lookouts. Civilians were being trained in defensive tactics, should the need arise. Our best warriors were gathered on adjoining beaches, readying themselves for battle.

Normally, as head warrior, I would've led those armies. Tonight, however, I had been summoned to the great chamber, a collapsed sea cave where our most important decisions were made, to meet with the Elders. I needed to share what I knew.

The Elders were all gathered in their seal forms at the top of the beach, where the water barely reached the rocks. None of us would dare change back to human form, which would make us too vulnerable when war was looming. I solemnly followed them into the great chamber, which was heavily guarded, and prepared to face their barrage of questions.

Their expressions were grim, much more than I'd ever seen before. Usually, we were a happy people. Jovial even in our old age. But tonight, the feeling of dread was palpable.

"Muir, come," Regani instructed. "Tell us about the witch man. Will he join in our fight?"

It was strange communicating telepathically with other Selkie after spending so much time communicating verbally in my human form. Images flew through my mind, each carrying urgent questions from Regani.

I bowed, which was the custom when a younger Selkie greeted an Elder. "I admit I am not certain. Tonight, I felt him, and he was reticent about joining our fight."

That caused quite a stir among the group. "Have you told him about his role, the reason you went to find him?" Caelan asked. His presence reinforced the critical urgency of this meeting with the Elders. As my second-in-command and the head warrior during my absence, he would be rejoining our armies as soon as possible.

"I have, yes, of course. And David came fully prepared to help us build our barriers back and avoid the humans, but neither of us knew the Dorcha would be threatening war."

"Have you told him of the pelt? That he, too, may be able to join us in the water?" Caelan asked. His mate might head the Council of Elders, but he held as much sway over our people as she did.

"No, I believed the time wasn't right. Our Dion Adair is unlike his predecessor. He doesn't have the same connection with magic. He accepted me as a Selkie, but he wasn't pleased when I referred to him as a witch."

The Elders paused as they processed that information. "Does he know how to use his powers?" one of the newer councilmembers asked. He had been accepted shortly before I left and was from a different clan than me, so I didn't know him well.

"I can only say the witches of a nearby village endowed him with a knowledge spell. He seems to be quite competent with that knowledge and harnessing its power."

"Muir, you must convince him to join us. Take the pelt of his ancestor with you and join him tonight and tell him, show him how much his skills are needed in this fight," Regani implored. I could hear the passion in her message. She was speaking for all our people.

I bowed again, knowing the conversation was concluded. I'd been given my orders and now must do what I could to convince David to go to battle for us, even if my heart hoped he'd leave and stay safe. The last war had almost wiped out both Selkie and Dorcha, and I had no doubt this one would do the same.

The youngest Elder followed me out and instructed a team of ten Selkie warriors to follow me back to Orkney. Through our connection, I knew David had rented a seaside cottage, and it was one I recognized. I'd seen it both from land and sea and was pleased I could go directly to him rather than have to transform and be at a disadvantage in the event the Dorcha attacked me.

I carried the Dion Adair's pelt in my mouth as I swam alongside the warriors toward the cottage. Upon reaching the shore, I instructed them to wait until I was inside before they left. I remained as a seal, scooted up to his door, and scratched, hoping he'd hear and let me in.

When David didn't come to the door, I tried to reach him through our connection and could tell he was asleep. I scratched again, trying to wake him, and this time I heard a noise from inside the cottage. He peered out of the door's tiny window, not seeing me, and didn't make a move to open it.

Just as I was about to scratch on the door again, it flew open, and I was splashed with a bucket full of water. I could hear the warriors behind me barking in laughter, and knew this would be a topic of conversation for many seasons.

I entered, using my tail to slap the door shut, and scooted past him into the living room. I laid down the Dion Adair's pelt on the sofa, removed my own, and transformed into my human form. "What was that for?" I asked, still dripping wet.

David's face was pale, and I realized he'd been afraid. "I thought if you were one of the Finfolk, then you'd be repelled by fresh water."

I stared at him for a moment, confused. "What is a Finfolk?"

"Oh, sorry, I meant Dorcha. The people here call them Finfolk, or at least used to call them that. They've been gone for a long time, but they were horrible enough that locals remember the stories."

I could sense David's tension easing, then he seemed to realize I was naked, because his eyes slowly raked over my body. I didn't mind the nudity, but I'd found that when I wasn't wearing clothing, David could get distracted, and tonight, we needed to stay on task. So, I went in search of a towel to dry off and the clothes he'd agreed to keep for me.

When I returned, David was sitting on the sofa, sipping a cup of tea, and staring at nothing in particular, lost in thought. "Are you okay?" I asked.

David shook his head. "No, I spotted a Dorcha just offshore after you and your Elders left. He was a scary sight, and it felt like I was being watched. I tried to sleep, but my head was filled with images of them, each more horrible than the last. They used to haunt these waters, terrifying the local villagers. Muir, can your people really defeat these monsters?"

I sat down next to him and put my hand on his knee. "We will need help. Lots of help."

David seemed to know what I was referring to and sighed. "I'm not a warrior, Muir. I'm barely even the witch you came seeking. In fact, I wouldn't be if it wasn't for the help of the Chemeketa people." I took his hand in mine. "I'd be more of a liability than an asset at this point."

"I seriously doubt that," I said, though I knew David's mind was already made up. Whether it was through our connection or just having come to know him as a person, I could feel his resolve before he even said anything.

I reached to my other side and picked up the pelt and placed it across his lap. "What's this, your pelt?" he asked. "Muir, I already told you, I have no interest in trapping you to stay with me."

"This isn't my pelt," I said, and held his gaze for several long moments. I could tell he was confused, so I continued. "David, this is the pelt that belonged to your ancestor, the Dion Adair's father and a true Selkie. It was worn by his son after his death, and we believe you will be able to wear it as well."

"You want me to become a Selkie?" His look held both amusement and curiosity.

"We don't know if it's possible, but your witch abilities combined with your Selkie ancestry may allow you to transform, if you want to."

David laughed nervously. "I'm barely a witch. I only know half of what I do because of the Chemeketa leaders, not because I'm special or some powerful being. I'm definitely not a seal. I'm sorry, Muir, this just isn't for me."

Sadness overwhelmed me, which I knew he could feel as well, but I decided not to let our final hours together be filled with disappointment or regret. I'd already known he was going to refuse, though hearing his words gave it finality. Despite all that had happened so far, and the undeniable connection we shared, he still couldn't–or wouldn't–allow anyone else to depend on him. He refused to see himself as a protector of anything but his own heart.

"My feelings for you are deep, deeper than I've ever felt for a lover. I understand your resolve. I'm disappointed, but I do understand. However, I have a duty to my people. I must join them in this fight. This war with the Dorcha could destroy the Selkie for eternity, and I can't let that happen."

I stood and turned away, hoping he couldn't see me as I wiped away a tear. Selkie weren't prone to strong emotions, and it was strange to have these feelings even in a human body, but my heart was truly breaking. I was going to lose David and nothing I could do would change his decision.

"Lie with me one last time," I said and held my hand out to him. David grasped it and stood, but didn't say a word as I led him to the bedroom. We stripped each other in silence, kissing and caressing as we went, then made love gently as the ocean crashed outside the window. I forced myself not to think of the Selkie warriors or the Dorcha that lurked beneath them. Tonight was for David and me alone.

I slipped out of the cottage and stole away into the predawn before David woke, eager not to attract the attention of any early risers who might otherwise catch me running across the beach naked as I transitioned back into my seal form. I carried the Dion Adair's pelt, which I now thought of as his, in my mouth as I swam away. With this last unsuccessful attempt, I would be returning it to the Elders.

David hadn't meant to, but in rejecting the pelt, he had also rejected his own heritage and a life with me. I wasn't sure which of those things hurt the most, but this was no longer the time for discussion or debate. A war was brewing. David would return to his home in Oregon, and I would resume my warrior duties and fight like hell to protect my people. Nothing could change that now.

# TWENTY-THREE

## DAVID

WHEN I WOKE, IT was to an empty bed. I knew Muir would leave and I knew he wouldn't wake me when he did. The pain was in his expression last night. I recognized it because it was the same pain I felt inside. But this war wasn't mine to fight. I was neither Selkie nor Dorcha.

I still wasn't convinced I was the witch he searched for. Sure, I was endowed with knowledge because of the people in Chemeketa, and I apparently came from a long line of witches on my birth father's side, but I was still just a man. I had little to no use for magic. I was a scientist, for goodness' sake—a simple man determined to live a simple life.

I regretted not being able to help Muir's people, but I was a peaceful man who believed in non-violence. If they were able to win this war, maybe I could return and shore up the boundaries as their Dion Adair had done before. That's what I'd come to do. That was all I could commit to doing.

I felt resolved, so why did it feel so wrong? I wasn't connected with the Selkie, and my ancestors hadn't been for at least a century or longer. And that was only if the stories Muir told me were to be believed. *It's possible I'm not descended from...* I stopped that line of thinking. Deep down, I knew what Muir had told me was the truth.

I had always been drawn to open water. From the first time I saw the ocean and smelled its salty sea air, I recognized its magic. Felt it. I possessed an uncanny ability to recognize sea life as well, even creatures I'd never learned about in school. We communed, as one of my marine biology mentors once told me. That's one reason I entered the field, and why I recognized Muir for what he was upon finding him injured in the sea cave. I had just never fully accepted my gifts and all they represented.

When Muir presented the Dion Adair's pelt to me, I sensed the pelt would accept me. I could feel my heart yearning for it. It called to me, spoke to me in a language I had never heard but fully understood. But instead of accepting it, and claiming my birthright, I used humor to deflect and cast it away.

The expression on Muir's face would be one I remembered for the rest of my life. Sadness permeated him, yet he was willing to let me go. He needed me, and not just as a lover, but as the savior of his people. But he hadn't manipulated me or spelled out the disaster that awaited his people without my help. Instead, he simply gave me my freedom.

It wasn't lost on me that I'd given him the same when we met. I had cured his pelt and rather than hide it, as I could've done to keep him with me, I had left it, ensuring him his freedom. I realized then that I hadn't declined the Dion Adair's pelt because I was a pacifist. No, in truth, I was afraid of the fight. How could I possibly hold my own against powerful sea creatures like the Dorcha? I'd been lucky just being able to fling one off a bridge back home, and even that had been with Muir's help.

My cowardice was certainly front and center, but what I feared more than anything, more than dying on a battlefield or, in this case, the depths of the ocean, was loving and losing. I feared I would lose Muir. And having given in to my fear, I'd actually lost him. How the hell had I not figured that out before now?

I slammed my teacup down on the counter and rushed out of the cottage into the early dawn. The sea's surface appeared unnervingly tranquil as I ran toward it. "Muir!" I yelled into the void.

I rushed into the water until the waves reached my waist. Had I been using my brain, I would've reached out to him using my powers rather than charging into open water. Instead, what came to meet me wasn't Muir, but the nightmare I'd had a few hours earlier.

The Nuckelavee leaped out of the water, grabbing me before I could even turn back. Pure anger poured through me. Nausea rose to meet it and I probably puked before I passed out. The last image in my mind as I slipped into unconsciousness was Muir's sweet face. A face I was sure I'd never see again.

# Twenty-Four

## Muir

"David!" I cried out in my mind as the link between us was severed. I felt the Dorcha attack him before everything—his mind, and our bond—went dark.

When I'd left him alone at the cottage, our connection was still strong. I'd hoped it would remain open, and that he'd change his mind. Now, I wasn't sure if he was alive or dead.

"I must find the Dion Adair! He's been attacked!" I announced to the warriors around me.

I immediately began swimming toward the shore, determined to find him. I had to know if he was alive. But my own warriors blocked my passage.

"The Elders want to see you, *now*," one burly warrior conveyed, leaving no room for dispute.

I knew not to disobey the Elders. I was angry and nearly frantic with worry, but I turned back and swam toward the great chamber.

"David has been hurt. The..." I blurted telepathically to the Elders, having forgone a customary bow in greeting, before Caelan stopped me.

I was ready for a dressing down for being disrespectful, but instead, he looked at me sadly and my mind interpreted the images he sent. "We know. We received reports just moments ago. The Dorcha took him. We have Selkie warriors following them but..." He shook his head. "Muir, this seems to have been their plan all along. The entire Dorcha contingent is disengaging. They are leaving our waters en masse."

"So, what? We let them take him? I'm why he's in this mess. They wouldn't have known about him if it weren't for me... for us!"

I searched the faces of the Elders and saw indecision. "I'll go for him myself. I can..."

"You won't," Regani said. "You will wait until we have thought this through, because getting yourself killed won't help him, and it will likely put him in greater danger."

I knew she was right, but I didn't want to hear logic. I only wanted David safe in my arms. I turned to leave, but the warriors once again blocked my way. That was too much, and I crumbled. "David is in danger. I must help him."

In an odd show of affection, Regani came over to where I sat and snuggled next to me. "You forget we still have the stone."

I looked up, hope filling me. "So, you'll help me find him?"

She turned back to the councilmembers and sighed. "We won't... can't leave him. Our destiny is tied to his. It has been since the first Dion Adair came to us. But you must trust us and allow us to decide how best to move forward."

She reached over and let her flipper slide down my back. "Trust us, Muir."

I felt the emotions flowing through me. I did trust them. I always had. The Elders had always worked hard to do what was best for our people. Even when we disagreed, we could not question their loyalty to our tribes.

"I do, and I will," I said before bowing in respect as I should've already done. Finally allowed to leave, I swam home to a small outcropping not far from the Elders' camp. I knew if I were left to my own thoughts, I'd go hunting for David. I wouldn't be able to stop myself. Being with my family might force me to think first. At least, I hoped it would.

# TWENTY-FIVE

## DAVID

I CONTINUED TO BE bombarded with images I didn't understand as another group of Dorcha appeared before me, clearly trying to communicate.

A colleague had once sent a video of a woman who believed she could communicate with large cats and that the communication came to her as images in her mind. It had been sent as a joke, but now, I couldn't help but think the woman had been onto something. That didn't make my current situation any better, though. When I didn't understand, the Dorcha abused me out of frustration. I'd been bitten, scratched, stabbed, and hit, but none of it helped me figure it out. As hard as I tried, I couldn't decipher the random images they sent me.

I had no idea where I was, somewhere underground. I'd been unconscious when I'd arrived, and the attacks had begun almost immediately after I woke up. I could smell the sea, and assumed I was in some sort of sea cave. All my powers seemed to have been depleted as well, and I felt nothing emanating from the sapphire bracelet clasped on my wrist.

Finally, after I puked for the third time since waking up thanks to a migraine causing me to feel more and more ill, the Nuckelavee returned and drove the rest of the Dorcha from the chamber.

It climbed out of the water and stared at me for a very long time. As I returned its unrelenting gaze, taking in the terrifying creature's partial horse-like appearance with fin-like flippers protruding from its legs, I wondered if this was my end. I had no doubt the pure hatred I'd felt when the Nuckelavee grabbed me could destroy me by itself or at least drive me mad.

After what felt like hours, it turned from me and leaped back into the water along the edge of the chamber. My injuries seemed superficial, but I hurt all over. There had to have been venom in a number of the bites and stings I had received, like from jellyfish or sea urchins. I doubted they were fatal, but the burning pain made it almost unbearable.

I managed to crawl to a small alcove and curled into as tight a ball as possible. Beyond that effort, I was too exhausted to move. Too tired to attempt an escape, even if I'd known how. More painful than my physical wounds, though, was *not* feeling my connection to Muir. He really was lost to me now, and for the first time in my life, I was truly alone.

Somehow, I managed to fall asleep, only to be woken some hours later for the process to begin all over again.

I had surveyed my surroundings, and all I could tell was that I was definitely in some sort of sea cave. The tides didn't seem to affect this area, so I could lie on the stone floor or escape into my little alcove when I wasn't being harassed by the Dorcha.

It felt as if days had passed, and with each one I became increasingly weaker. The Dorcha continued their communication efforts, but their images became less and less focused in my head. Either they didn't understand human anatomy or didn't care, because they had yet to feed me or give me fresh water. The only thing that kept me from dying of dehydration was a few drops of fresh water that dripped from a wall in the alcove.

If only I had my powers, I was sure I could've healed my wounds, or used the Chemeketa people's knowledge to formulate some plan of defense or escape. But somehow, the Dorcha had blocked all my powers. I was becoming hopeless. Every moment I spent in the cave, the cold settled deeper into my bones. My thirst grew so strong it was as if I were going mad. I knew the elements and the never-ending injuries would eventually do me in. I just wished I had gone with Muir when he'd asked instead of getting in my own way.

He was who I thought about as I lay dying in that alcove. I'd said this wasn't my battle, but I'd been wrong. This *was* my war, as it was for all other humans whether they knew it or not. I might not be able to interpret the images the Dorcha sent me, but the message was still abundantly clear. These creatures hated humans, and would delight in our complete annihilation. In many ways, the only thing standing in their way were the Selkie.

I didn't know what these creatures had planned, but if their treatment of me was any indication, it was going to be horrible for anyone or anything in their path. I closed my eyes and for the hundredth time let the tears flow for the love I'd let slip through my fingers. If by some miracle

I made it out of this cave alive, I would never take my abilities, my heritage, or my love of Muir for granted ever again.

# TWENTY-SIX

## MUIR

MY FAMILY CONSOLED ME, and my younger siblings tried to cheer me up as I waited to hear from the Elders. I yearned for David, my emotions fluctuating between anger at myself for not making him see his need to join us and despair that I hadn't stayed to protect him.

When the Elders finally summoned me, I was extremely anxious. I swam as quickly as I could to the Elders' beach. I scanned their faces to see if I could decipher what they'd decided. The only thing I could tell was that they were all exhausted.

"Muir," Regani said in greeting. "We've reached a decision about the Dion Adair."

She turned, mentally checking with the other Elders before continuing. "After much long debate, we all agree that it must be you and a few hand-picked warriors who rescue the Dion Adair. We can, if we combine our powers, hide you from the Dorcha's attention. But Muir, that's about all we can do to help. If you're captured, we cannot send rescue."

I nodded and turned to pick my warriors, but halted when Regani flooded my mind with more images. "Muir, this is a suicide mission," she conveyed. "Know that before you choose your warriors. It's unlikely any of you will return."

I turned to face her and bowed. "I will go alone. As you've said, this is a suicide mission. I won't be able to fight my way through, even with additional warriors. It'll be stealth and speed I depend on, so traveling solo will be an advantage."

She nodded as if she already knew that would be my answer. "Then take the Dion Adair's stone and pelt," she said as she nudged both toward me with her nose. "You need to keep the stone on you at all times. It will lead you to your lover once again."

That caught me by surprise. I hadn't told the Elders that David and I were lovers. Not that they would've cared. Casual coupling wasn't something we concerned ourselves with. But when a Selkie took a lover, it was considered significant. And Regani was right about David. He was in all ways but formally my love. My mate.

I nodded and transformed back into my human form, placing the stone at my throat, where I'd placed it when I began my quest so long ago. Images of David's whereabouts immediately filled my mind.

There was something different this time when the stone touched my human skin, though. I could feel the Elders' protection, and I knew they were putting themselves at risk. A Selkie couldn't swim among other marine life without the ability to ward off predators. Somehow the Elders had embedded their powers into the stone. Now, not only could I avoid natural predators, but I would be able to do the same with the Dorcha.

I wanted to ask, would they get their powers back if I failed? But the way the Elders looked at me told me no. No, they would never regain their powers of self-protection unless I returned with the stone. I placed the stone back on the ground. "This is too much. It's too dangerous. If you are lost and the council is no more, all the Selkie would be at risk."

Each of the Elders shifted then. Sitting in their human forms on their designated rocks, their pelts draped over their laps, they looked otherworldly. "If you fail, Muir, we are as good as dead anyway," Caelan said aloud. "Without the Dion Adair, we are all the more vulnerable to humans and Dorcha. It would only be a matter of time before our extinction."

"Muir," Regani interrupted. "We did not make this decision lightly. You are one of the most powerful warriors we have. You are also in love with the Dion Adair. You are the best bet for saving our people, so we unanimously decided to give what little power we have to you. We know you will do all you can to return safely and bring our protector with you."

The humility of my leaders touched me. They had each put their trust in me again, just as they had done in assigning me my initial quest. But, this time, their commitment was personal. They had placed their lives in my hands.

I reached down, picked the stone back up, and bowed before them. Placing the stone at my throat, I slipped my pelt back on, took the Dion Adair's pelt in my mouth, and dove into the water. Letting the stone guide me, I swam as hard and fast as I could toward the man I loved—the man who held my heart and the fate of my people in his hands.

# TWENTY-SEVEN

## DAVID

I WAS IN AND out of consciousness. The Dorcha had thankfully stopped torturing me. Occasionally, one would crawl out of the water and stare at me for ages, then disappear, only to be replaced with another one.

In my feverish state, I felt the desperation in their stares. As if they needed me to understand. But that could just be my dying mind making up stories to justify my impending mortality.

Finally, even those strange visits stopped, and I was left alone, curled in a ball, waiting to die.

When something nudged me awake, I immediately recoiled, afraid I was once again going to be inflicted with intense pain. But when nothing bit, poked or scratched me, I cracked an eye open.

Seeing Muir's beautiful face just inches from my own brought a surge of intense happiness. Joy I'd never felt before filled me. I tried to talk, but I was too weak, and my words came out as a low murmur. Muir's eyes darted around the cave before he began stripping me out of my clothes.

I must've dozed off as he struggled to undress me. I was completely naked when he gently shook me awake and whispered, "You must put on the pelt, my love. It'll bring you some strength. Goddess willing, it will work."

I looked down at the pelt in his hand, and just like before, I felt its pull, a yearning from deep within.

Muir slipped the top over my head, and the rest of the pelt fell freely, even eagerly, over my body. At the same time, I felt my wrist grow warm as my grandmother's bracelet absorbed into my skin, as if it had become a part of me as well. One moment, I was human, and the next, I was... a seal. I looked over in time to see Muir change as well.

Just as he had said, the pelt brought a new level of energy. I still felt fatigued, but I was at least able to move. I opened my mouth to speak and immediately saw images in my mind not unlike what the Dorcha had been sending me.

This time, maybe because they were from Muir, or because I now wore the pelt, I could understand them. It was almost like the images were being translated into English in my mind, and the conversion was instant.

"We need to leave, but you'll have to stay close to me. Really close. I think the stone will keep us both disguised, but I honestly don't know for sure," he said. I was still reeling from my new ability to understand the images flowing into my mind. Delirium also still played a part, so I only caught some of what I heard. Or was it saw?

He nudged me toward the water, and when I dived in, he followed closely, nudging me forward. I could sense the Dorcha around us, but they didn't seem to know we were there.

We swam silently for several moments when a whale breached, momentarily separating us.

I immediately felt the Dorcha swimming toward me. Muir rushed to my side, but it was too late, we were surrounded. This time as the images swept through my mind, I understood them. The messages were dark, desperate, as if from an injured animal trapped in a cage.

Muir moved between me and the Nuckelavee. "Leave him alone," he demanded of the Dorcha.

"He belongs to us now," the Nuckelavee snapped.

I didn't even need to understand them to feel the intense anger being leveled at us from all sides. I recognized the creatures who surged toward us as the ones who'd tortured me in the cave. Without a thought, I cast out a spell that flung them all back, stunning them.

Muir rammed into me, forcing me to swim through the temporary opening my spell had created. I could feel the rage as the Dorcha regained their full senses, but I had no fear. Donning the pelt had clearly made me more powerful, and sheer instinct informed me how to wield it.

For the first time in my life, I felt completely at ease with myself. As if I was finally who I'd been meant to be all along. Part human, part witch, part Selkie.

To Muir's dismay, I stopped swimming and turned back to face the Dorcha. "Stop!" I demanded, and with the command sent a shockwave of power that halted their pursuit.

"You've captured me, tortured me, almost killed me, but I have regained my strength and my powers. You can no longer harm me. Go now, vacate these waters immediately. If you return or attempt to harm any Selkie under my protection, I will destroy you."

I felt their collective dismay, and the emotion confused and bewildered me. I figured they'd be angry or disappointed. Surely their intention in kidnapping me was somehow related to the war. Regardless, before I could inquire, the Dorcha turned as one and swam away.

Muir, who had remained solidly at my side, nudged me forward again. We swam a long way, my body becoming stronger and stronger the further we got from the Dorcha and the ever-present sense of darkness among them. We came to rest on the shore of a small, uninhabited island for the night. Muir appeared to be in protective warrior mode, which I had to admit was hot as hell, and wanted to remain on guard, but I convinced him I was strong enough now to take part of the watch so he could sleep.

By morning we were both rested enough to continue our journey. It took almost another day to reach the island that held the Elders' beach. Muir had spent the day telling me through images everything that happened since I'd been kidnapped. How he'd felt our connection break, and how the Elders had sacrificed their personal protection to magically keep Muir hidden as he searched for me.

By the time we reached the Elders, I was significantly more impressed with them than before, and grateful.

They welcomed us into their great chamber, as Muir called it, but I stayed in the water in my seal form as he climbed out and removed his pelt. He then removed the stone from around his neck and placed it onto what appeared to be a makeshift altar made from one of the boulders that'd fallen when the ancient sea cave collapsed.

Each of the Elders shed their pelts and walked toward the altar. A dark blue glow emanated from the stone and split apart into separate streams that flowed back into each person.

Somehow, perhaps from the knowledge I'd absorbed by wearing the pelt, I knew the act rendered the once powerful stone useless. The Elders had sacrificed themselves to save me, and the sapphire had also sacrificed itself in being the instrument to make that happen.

*Magic requires sacrifice.* The distant voices of the Chemeketa people flickered through my mind as a single, unified image. That was a lesson I would remind myself never to forget.

Once the Elders and Muir returned to their seal forms, Muir beckoned to me. I climbed out of the water and came to his side. "Welcome, Dion Adair. We've awaited your arrival for a very long time."

I bowed instinctively, and when I lifted my head, I watched as the Elders fell back, forming a path to the high rock on which they had all been seated. My instincts told me it was a place of power, and the invitation to ascend the stone throne was clearly a mark of respect for my position as the Dion Adair. The weight of the honor bestowed on me caused me to feel overcome with emotions, I climbed up and took my place among the Selkie leaders.

# Twenty-Eight

## Muir

ONCE DAVID CLAIMED HIS rightful place as the Dion Adair, the Elders spent hours upon hours talking to him about Selkie issues. The most pressing of which was what to do if the Dorcha returned. David sat silently, listening to the Elders express their opinions, and I chuckled as Regani eventually took her position back on the head rock. He might be our protector, but she knew how to run the council. David made eye contact with me and silently acknowledged that Regani should be in charge right now.

I snickered to myself, knowing David didn't care about status. Why would he? We all knew and could feel the power radiating from him now that the pelt had accepted him. As the discussion slowly shifted from issues that pertained to David and me to more mundane things, like helping get the community back to normal, exhaustion caught up with us both. David respectfully bowed toward the council before informing them we were leaving to go rest.

That night, as David and I lay together as seals on the beach, watching the moon as she crossed the night sky,

I thanked the goddess for my good fortune. David was mine, our people were safe, and our borders would soon be secure... I just didn't know for how long.

# Twenty-Nine

## David

OVER THE NEXT FEW weeks, I could feel myself becoming more powerful by the day. The idea that *absolute power corrupts absolutely* was never far from my thoughts. The weight of my responsibility to the Selkie and people of Chemeketa kept me grounded, though, not that I'd ever craved power anyway. Muir and I speculated on whether I'd acquired the previous Dion Adair's witch power in the same way he'd acquired his father's Selkie power upon donning the pelt, but even the Elders were at a loss for certainty on the matter.

Before long, Muir and I fell into a routine. I'd join the Elders for meetings, which at times felt endless no matter how efficiently Regani ran them, while Muir occupied his time training with the warriors. Thankfully, the nights belonged to us alone. I became his eager student on making love in the ocean, but sometimes we'd transform into humans to have sex on the beach. I didn't have a preference on form, I simply craved being with him.

Muir commented on the changes within me since the pelt accepted me. He was right. I was very much still myself, but the fears, especially those around my gifts, had all but vanished. Also, my reservations about love caused by my birth father's curse had subsided. I assumed it had something to do with my transformation from human to Selkie.

I was thankful the role I'd taken among the Elders was more symbolic than obligatory. I mostly listened with one ear during our regular council meetings, picking up only the important details, since I couldn't care less which type of fish they should focus on as the currents changed or how many pups should be allowed to take their walkabout each year.

What did interest and concern me was the failing protection barriers of the last Dion Adair. Of course, that's why Muir had found me, and I'd come all this way. Not to become a leader of the Selkie Council of Elders. I'd recently inspected the boundaries and found them disintegrating. When I tried to reinforce them, my energies quickly drained away. Marta's lessons, more than the other knowledge I'd acquired, reminded me I was using the wrong methods for reinforcing them.

I experimented daily using different energies, pulling from each element first, then from aspects of the landscape around me. I even used the combined energies of the Selkie, and not even that helped.

I was at a loss. I began having dreams of the moon or the goddess within. Sometimes she'd even visit in her human form, but she offered no answer to my dilemma.

Some nights I'd dream of my predecessor, the first Dion Adair, and tried to ask him questions. But he never responded, just smiled knowingly.

After what had to be months, I was lying on the rocks just this side of the boundary when a pup's head poked above the water. The toddler climbed onto the rocks beside me and began peppering me with questions.

I chuckled, answering while scanning the water's surface for his parents. Finally, I interrupted the inquisition and asked where they were.

He looked at me curiously and before I could ask again, light burst from the pup. Within moments, I found myself lying in front of a man who, judging by his attire, appeared to be an ancient wizard.

I scrambled up, ready to either flee or defend myself, when the man put up a hand to stop me. "You have nothing to fear, Dion Adair. I am friend, not foe." Although he now appeared in human form, the old man continued communicating telepathically.

"Who are you?" I asked.

The man chuckled. "I am the source of the power inside you," he said.

"The Selkie?" I asked. I'd seen the former Dion Adair in my dreams and knew this wasn't him. I was confused.

The old man shook his head. "I am the first to hold the power of the fairy people. The first half-human, half-Fae."

"W-why have you come to me?" I asked, stammering with nerves that were still frayed from the Selkie pup's shocking transformation.

"Because you called to me."

For the life of me, I had no idea what he was talking about. "Um, when did I call for you?"

He stared at me for a long time before he answered. "You called to me first when you lay in the cave of the

Dorcha. Then again when you transformed into a seal. And most recently when you were dreaming of how to rebuild the Selkie boundaries."

I still couldn't remember calling on the old wizard, but I could certainly use help rebuilding the boundaries. The possibility excited me.

"How? How do I fix them?" I asked, but I had no sooner spoken than the old man had disappeared.

In his place was the Nuckelavee. I immediately pulled up my powers, ready to attack. "Not all things are as they seem," the Nuckelavee said, and I knew it was still the old man, not a Dorcha.

"Can you help me with the boundary or not?" I asked, annoyed with the games the man was playing.

"I have already helped you. Not all things are as they seem, and not all things that served in the past will serve in the future. Things change, young one, and will continue to change as long as the Earth moves through the skies. You must learn to look beyond what's apparent, to see what is."

I'd always hated riddles, and that's all I heard in the old man's words. *Just spit it out already.* I turned to him to say as much, but he was gone.

I shook my head to make sure I wasn't just imagining it all. When I was sure he wouldn't return, I slipped off my rock and swam back toward the Elders' beach. I needed to share with them what I'd seen. Maybe they would have some insight into what it all meant.

***

The second full moon came and went since I'd taken up residence with the Selkie, and I was no closer to providing them protection.

It was the day of that full moon when the precarious nature of our situation made itself abundantly clear.

I had taken up my usual spot on the rocks just outside the Elders' beach when I heard the sounds of men laughing from above. When I looked up, sheer terror filled me.

Four men were rappelling down the cliff wall and into the collapsed cave that housed the great chamber.

I barked a warning, and all ten of the Elders on the beach looked up at once. They rushed from their rocks and dove into the sea while I took up guard alongside the warriors charged with their security.

As soon as all four men landed, more quickly followed until a total of eleven men sat on the sacred rocks of the Elders. They were laughing and teasing one another, passing around beer cans and making a huge ruckus, not even remotely aware of the impact their presence had on the Selkie, not to mention the disrespect to the Elders.

This was a sacred place of power. Not even regular Selkie were allowed into the collapsed cave of the Elders, and here these men were getting sloshed on sacred ground with little regard to nature or the creatures around them. For the first time in my life, I felt some of the anger that had radiated from the Dorcha. As the men openly defiled the sacred stones, I began to understand the words of the old wizard. *Not all things are as they seem.*

Before nightfall, the drunken men rappelled back up the side of the cliff, leaving most of their empty beer cans behind. That night, the Elders returned to the great chamber and declared the protective boundaries officially defunct. I tried to help the warriors remove the litter, but was stopped.

"No," Caelan said, pulling me aside. "You must be seen as an authority. Now your position here is more important than ever. We must either find a way to shore up our boundaries or find another solution altogether. But, Dion Adair, our time is running out. There is another collapsed sea cave not far from here, and the humans use it daily during the summer months. It's just a matter of time before every beach we have to ourselves will be lost, and we will all be exposed and at risk."

I nodded, feeling inadequate given my inability to solve the problem. I swam through the waters and back to Muir. I would need his support now more than ever as I faced this dilemma.

# THIRTY

## MUIR

"**N**O ONE BLAMES YOU, David," I said, trying to console him. He'd been distraught the night the men defiled the Elders' beach. David had stopped attending the council meetings and instead went daily to where the boundary used to be and tried casting spell after spell to reinstate it.

Everyone could see his efforts were in vain, and the days of our guaranteed protection were gone.

With the removal of the boundaries, human tourists came to occupy beaches long reserved for Selkie. Most recently, two of our pups had been chased and almost caught by dogs as tourists moored their boats and came ashore with their animals.

The danger increased daily as the summer progressed. More and more humans meant fewer and fewer safe places for us. "It'll improve over the winter," I tried reassuring David one night after another dog chased a Selkie family from their home.

"Then what? They return the following summer in even greater numbers. I'm no use here, Muir. I'm not helping anyone!"

I went to console him, but David shook me off and took to the water. The connection we'd had since we first met had only grown stronger since David's pelt accepted him. I could sense where he was at all times even without the stone, which was why I let him go even as he swam further away than ever.

Everything within me said David needed to be alone. He needed to process everything and find within himself whatever was missing in order to use his powers to the fullest and save our people.

Still, I worried about him. Not that any harm would befall him, since even the most ferocious sea creatures wouldn't dare approach, but I worried for his sense of self. I could feel his anguish and as much as I wanted to help alleviate it, I no more had the knowledge or power to do so than he did to rebuild the boundary at this point.

# Thirty-One

## David

I HAD NO REAL destination in mind as I swam through the sea. I crossed a shipping route Muir and the Elders had warned me not to cross, unable to stop myself for some reason. The huge ships were daunting, and I dove deep to avoid being hit by their giant propellers.

I swam until I reached an island and pulled myself onto the shore, where I finally allowed myself to sleep. I dreamed of the Dorcha. They'd followed me since I'd left Muir, but I was no longer afraid of them. They no longer posed a threat to me.

My dreams, though, were disturbing. I had a vision of two Dorcha children who'd been seriously injured and were wailing in pain. When another figure appeared, silent and floating on the surface, I immediately knew a third child hadn't survived. At first, I couldn't tell what had caused their injuries, but the culprit became clear when three giant male orca attacking boats off the coast of New England came into view.

The dreams shifted to similar scenes of carnage involving Dorcha being maimed or killed. One dream showed a group of fishermen indiscriminately hunting sea creatures simply for sport and tossing them all back into the water either mortally wounded or already dead.

I woke up with a headache and a full understanding of what my distant ancestor had been trying to tell me. The same thing I'd glimpsed when I'd seen the men climb into the Elders' sacred space. *Not all things are as they seem*.

The revelation was so strong it made my stomach hurt. Was it possible that the Dorcha might not be the evil entities we thought they were? In fact, could they be victims of the same thing the Selkie were trying to overcome?

The next day, I continued swimming away from the Selkie homeland. I was still unsure where I was going, but I felt the pull to continue until I found answers. What I eventually found, though, a floating pile of plastic. As I swam through the rubbish, I had to stop multiple times to rescue aquatic animals caught up in the mess. Fishing nets choked turtles and needlessly killed fish and even mammals.

The longer I spent in the plastic wasteland, the more it felt like a floating hell. I finally got past it and arrived at yet another island, littered with trash, everything from plastic bottles to used diapers.

I was tired and had to sleep on the dirty island. My entire body rebelled at being forced to rest there.

That night, my dreams were filled with beaches where turtles could no longer lay their eggs, shorelines where birds could no longer nest, and vast coastal areas that were dead due to human pollution.

I saw images of the red tide along America's southeast coastal regions, of remarkable creatures like the manatee either disappearing or on the brink. The entire ocean was at risk.

Which meant all life was at risk.

I felt rather than saw the presence of the Nuckelavee climbing onto the shore where I slept. I rose to meet him, remembering the torture I'd endured at his people's hands.

This time, the images he sent me weren't difficult to understand. "We need help. We are dying and can't survive much longer."

I angrily thrust images of my repeated assaults back at him. Images of being bitten, stabbed, poked, and the burning pain caused by their stinging poison. "How dare you ask for my help when you almost killed me."

His response shocked me. "We didn't think a witch could die. We thought you were holding out on us, trying to avoid helping us."

I detected no malice in his words. I knew he was telling the truth. "How did you disable my powers.

Apparently, it had something to do with the cave itself. He was unsure why it suppressed the powers of a witch, but it suppressed their own as well. They couldn't shapeshift when they were in the cave.

He showed me images of how the cave was used by the Dorcha leaders to meet and discuss important issues because it forced them to be honest, having rendered them unable to use latent powers to evade the truth.

I chuckled at that despite myself. In that way, the Dorcha were the same as human leaders. Too bad humans didn't have a way to force politicians to tell the truth when important decisions needed to be made.

"Will you help us?" the Nuckelavee asked. "Can you help us survive before we are wiped out forever?"

I thought for a moment, remembering the stories Muir had told me of their origins. "You can no longer avoid human contact or hunt or scare them. The more you provoke them, the more danger you put your people in."

The Nuckelavee nodded. "We've already learned that. We have not provoked the humans in over a century, yet they become more dangerous as the years pass."

"And what of your war with the Selkie?"

"We never wanted war," he said, all but interrupting me. "We wanted *you*."

I sighed. "I will consider what you've asked, but I cannot make any guarantees. If I need to speak to you again, how can I find you?"

"I will stay close. Just reach out, and I will come."

With that, the sea creature, one I surprisingly no longer felt was the monster of myth, slipped back amongst the waves and disappeared.

I stared at the water. I was no closer to answering my question about securing the boundary, but I did have a better understanding of the Dorcha and their needs.

I also knew it was time to return to Muir. Time to return to the islands and resume my place among the Elders, informing them of all I'd learned. I was still dubious about the Dorcha, but after my dreams and the visit from my wizard ancestor, I knew what he had said was true. *Not all things are as they seem*. The Dorcha were not the enemy the Selkie believed them to be.

It took longer to get back than it had to get away. I had to swim against the currents, which exhausted me much faster than I had anticipated. Each night, however, when I needed refuge, I found a small island or a piece of floating debris, something that enabled me to climb out of the water and rest.

When I caught a glimpse of the ancient standing stones on the shores of Orkney as I swam past the island, something connected within me. The answers I sought would be found there. I was suddenly sure of that. Knowledge from the Chemeketa leaders informed me just enough to know I would need to conduct a proper ritual for the stones to speak to me.

I now had direction. I would seek knowledge from the standing stones, and if I was truly the destined leader everyone hailed me as, I'd get the Selkie to help me do it.

# THIRTY-TWO

## MUIR

DAVID LIFTED HIS HANDS to the sky. Lightning flashed, lighting up our faces as he chanted a ritual he only knew because of the Chemeketa people. After the flash and the eerie quiet that followed—lightning without thunder always struck me as odd—magic began to flow around the circle.

As the power reached us, we, too, began to chant in a language that hadn't been spoken by a Selkie in centuries. But somehow, through David, we all knew and understood the words.

*"Waters in which we dwell, Land from which we come...*

*Pour upon us thy wisdom and guidance."*

That's roughly what it translated to. At least in my mind.

With our collective chanting, the standing stones began to glow and the area beyond the stones started to blur. Thanks to a series of spells David had cast using his collective Chemeketa knowledge, no one would be able to see us within the stone circle. We were invisible from the outside.

David threw his head back, and a light began to glow from the center of his chest, pulsing with each heartbeat. As the light grew stronger, it separated into streams before taking on the shape of three people. A very old man with a long beard carrying a staff. A Selkie in human form with long dark hair that blew around his face as if a great wind were accosting him. And another man we'd never seen before but recognized the instant he appeared.

We had felt his energy every day of our lives. The one who had set the boundaries around our homeland waters and saved us all those years ago. Our legendary Dion Adair.

The Dion Adair stepped forward and bowed before the Elders. "You were wise to summon us, great leaders, for we sense you are facing great danger."

The Selkie man stepped forward next and laid his hand on the Dion Adair's shoulder. "I am your Dion Adair's father. I, too, have been summoned to help you on this night."

Finally, the old man stepped between the two. "I am..." The name he spoke was too foreign to my ears to understand. A name that held immense power. "I am the first of the human and northern Fae to be born on this land."

The old man waved his hand, and we watched as images raced across the stone circle. Magical creatures that once walked this land and swam in these waters flashed before our eyes, then disappeared just as quickly. The scenes only lasted moments, but the history of magic in the human world since the time of the fairies was now etched in all our minds.

The three stood side by side in front of David, whose back was still arched with his hands thrust in front of him, manifesting his three predecessors who were a part of him.

"You all must leave this land," the Dion Adair told us. "The ancient power in these stones has grown too weak to hold the magic required to protect you. Trust your new Dion Adair to lead you safely. Seek the place where the Fae escaped to long ago, where you can be safe as well."

The circle of Selkie grew restless. I, too, felt the impact of the Dion Adair's words. Leave our homeland? What of the great chamber, and the pups' *coisich mun cuairth*? The land and waters we'd always occupied were a part of us. Who would we be as Selkie without it?

The Selkie man stepped forward then, and said, "You may remain creatures of the sea in this new land, but you must integrate into the human and witch society. Never again must you allow the elements, culture, or fear separate you from your human cousins."

That created an even greater stir. It was one thing to leave the places we'd always known, but another to integrate with a society of humans. How would that work?

The old man stepped forward and with a wave of his hand, calm settled around us. We all turned to him to hear what he had to say.

"For generations, you have been at war with the ones you call Dorcha. They have also fought the humans and thus were cursed by my mother, Queen of the northern Fae. That curse will end this day, for you will need each other if you wish to survive. Your Dion Adair–" The old man gestured behind him, indicating David. "–has spoken with the leader of the Dorcha. He will guide the reconnection of both groups. You have been enemies for longer than you have been in the sea, but your alliance is your key to salvation."

Bravely, Regani stepped forward, and asked, "How can any of these things possibly happen? Surely, this is more change than a small group of Selkie can endure and survive."

The old man sighed, but held firm. "Our descendant called to us for guidance and that is what we offer. Heed this warning. If you refuse the instructions we have given you tonight, your existence on this earth will end. This is the only path we can foresee in which the Selkie survive."

"Must all of us leave? Or can some stay here on our ancestral land?" I asked, stunned to hear the question leave my lips.

The three looked at one another inquisitively as if silently communicating. Finally, after several stressful moments, the old man said, "Enough magic remains to conceal a small contingent of warriors, at least for a short time. But for their safety, no one else should stay behind for long, and none can stay forever."

As he finished speaking, the ghostly Dion Adair lifted his hands and called out into the night. I felt the energy shift and knew the boundaries had been restored, at least to some degree.

Without further discussion, the three began to fade, their magical forms absorbed by David. As soon as the light reflected from them had disappeared, David collapsed.

I immediately rushed to his side and cradled his head as he lay unconscious.

"We must return home and consider what we have learned tonight. Muir, bring the Dion Adair with you," Regani stated. "When he is fully rested, bring him before the Elders to discuss how we go forward."

The magic protecting the stone circle dissipated, and my people hurried toward the ocean, each carrying their pelt and talking in hushed whispers.

The news shared with us by David's ancestors was daunting, and I admit I was feeling alarmed.

I lifted David in my arms, carried him to the shore, slipped his pelt back onto his body, and placed him on a raft of driftwood we'd hidden on the beach. When I transformed myself, I used my nose to nudge the raft toward home.

As I swam, I absently wondered what we'd be facing had I not ventured on my quest. David brought huge changes to my people, but with it came opportunity. We had sought him out and asked for his help, and no matter how daunting it seemed, our only hope was to abide by his words and those of his ancestors. I just hoped the Elders would agree.

# THIRTY-THREE

## DAVID

I'D BEEN HALF AWAKE when my ancestors appeared through me to speak with the Selkie. It felt like an out-of-body experience. I could see what was happening, but was more of an observer than participant.

I'd suspected when I began to chant the words that came into my head from Crystal, a Chemeketa witch who specialized in chants and rituals, that something like that would happen. I'd hoped the standing stones would simply reveal what needed to happen, but that would've been too easy. Now, as my ancestors had made clear, the fate of the Selkie, and even the Dorcha, rested squarely on my shoulders, and that weight of responsibility felt heavy.

I could hear the ruckus before I arrived at the Elders' beach. It seemed the entire Selkie population was gathered there and all of them, young and old, were arguing.

Silence fell upon my arrival, making me more than a little self-conscious. Muir sat with the warriors, as was required because of his rank, while I took my place among the Council of Elders.

He'd told me to expect contention among the group. "You must be impartial. If any Selkie choose to stay, you must allow them to make that decision. If you seem too eager to get them to follow you, they'll assume it's a trap."

I faced the Selkie alone. I had to do this on my own. I was the Dion Adair, an outsider but also their protector. I couldn't be seen as influenced even by my lover. Too much was at stake for these people, and all I had to offer them as guidance was a vast knowledge of magic that wasn't my own, and of course, a degree in marine biology that probably wasn't much help in this circumstance. I had no expertise in relocating an entire people, much less ripping them from their homeland, bridging century-old disputes, or finding a safe place for them to live where they could integrate into the human race.

The task ahead seemed so daunting I almost turned around and fled, but we all knew just how dire the circumstances were. Either I would help save these people, or their existence would not be long for this world.

Regani slid from her perch and indicated I was to take her place. I'd been thinking about what to say since I woke up from the spellcasting. The only thing I could come up with was asking them to remember the images my ancestors had shared during the ritual at the stone circle. Disturbing images of the extermination of so many magical creatures wiped out through the centuries.

I lifted my body, so I displayed my full seal authority, then began, "When the fairies still occupied this land, many human Fae came to descend from them. Ancient tree shepherds long ago vanished as human populations grew larger and stronger." I let the memory of great forests slashed and burned take shape in the minds of the Selkie. Today, the British Isles had been so deforested it was almost unrecognizable from what it'd been just a few centuries ago.

"The fairy folk left our lands long ago, and those of us who bear the blood of both humans and Fae have been forced to remain in this dimension. Few of our kind are left, and the numbers of Selkie and your Dorcha cousins diminishes annually. We are faced with the reality of extinction, and you must now decide the fate of the magical sea folk. Will you embrace the advice of my ancestors, or will you allow Selkie and Dorcha to disappear from this earth forever?"

I'd reached the end of what I'd come up with as my argument. I knew I could go into detail about climate change, talk about changing sea currents, and discuss issues I'd written about in my dissertation, but as creatures of the sea, they understood the changes on a deeper level than I ever could.

The Selkie knew the odds against them. There was no question about that. So, I sat on the top of the Elders' rock and listened to their collective silence, a silence that spoke louder than any words.

"When would we have to go?" a young female in the crowd asked.

"That should be decided by the Elders, but I can only caution that the boundaries are no longer in place. The Dion Adair who came to you last night was only able to secure a small section, but only for a short time."

"Who gets to stay?" an elderly man asked from the back of the crowd.

Regani came forward, and replied, "That must still be debated, but without the same boundary protections we've had in the past, it is likely only those too old to make the journey and a group of warriors to protect them will remain behind."

I looked at the leader then, and added, "Once we're settled, I have friends who may be willing to give the elderly, infirm, and families with young children passage in their human form to the new settlement." I was speaking for the folk in Chemeketa, but I wanted to ensure I wasn't making a promise they wouldn't keep but still give hope that we wouldn't be leaving anyone behind.

That caused a stir, although I thought it was more because my proposal would require the elderly remove their pelts, making them even more vulnerable than they already were.

"And what of the Dorcha? How can we trust them? They will lead us to the depths and murder us," the warrior next to Muir said.

I sighed. "I can't speak for the Dorcha. They must do that for themselves. I've met with their leader, and despite the actions their past, I believe they wish for a truce. And, more importantly, they understand the stakes."

I looked out over the gathered Selkie, huddled together, looking sad or scared, and my heart went out to them. They were strangely calm, but I could feel their anxiety. I would've preferred arguing and fighting to eliminate the hopelessness that seemed to be coming from them.

"You have lived here separated from the rest of the world. The currents bring you fish, although not as much as in the past. You've had to face shipping routes, but they are predictable, and you've been able to avoid them. The Dorcha haven't had the same level of security, and as a result, they've seen the uglier, scarier elements of life in today's oceans." I paused to glance among the group, and seeing a few heads nodding in understanding, I continued, "Let me propose this. I will speak with the Elders and, if they agree, we will appoint a group of Selkie warriors as emissaries to speak with the Dorcha. Let them begin discussing how Selkie and Dorcha can work together and, eventually, live together in harmony. I believe they are worried too. I've seen the world they've had to fight to survive in and know it's been challenging. I'm asking you to make the effort before deciding you can't trust them and sealing all your fates."

"But the ancestor said if we didn't go, we wouldn't survive. How is that a choice?" another young woman asked.

"He did, and I agree with him, but ultimately, the decision must be yours to make. Leaving is a choice, as is staying here."

"Living with humans, though? How is that even possible?" she countered.

I shook my head. "I don't know the answer to that. Muir has told me you have all spent time on land in your human form. That means you have experienced being amongst humans in one way or another. But in terms of integrating into their society, that's something you must work out for yourselves."

Just like that, everyone began talking again, and I knew my part was over. As I slid off the rock, Regani came over and thanked me. "You did well," she said. "Now, we must let the people come to terms with what has been said. I'm afraid nothing about this will be fast."

"I'm a patient man, I can wait. But I will warn you, it'll be easier to ignore the warnings and look in the other direction. You and the other Elders should put a time limit on the discussions and make a final decision soon. All of you are at risk. The sooner you decide how to proceed, the sooner we can get you to safety."

The Elder nodded and said, "You are wise, Dion Adair. Thank you for your counsel."

With that, I was effectively dismissed from the meeting, so I slid back into the water, and this time was mostly ignored as I swam back to my beach. The Selkie needed time to debate and process everything, and as much as I was enjoying my time with them, I was still an outsider. Never before had that been more apparent than it was today.

Upon reaching the secluded beach Muir and I called home, I transitioned back into my human form and rubbed at my wrist and the sapphire bracelet I'd inherited from my grandmother. I hadn't even considered using the bracelet to call my grandmother even though she'd told me I could. But now, my loneliness was so intense I wanted any contact, even that of a ghost.

As I closed my eyes and called her image to mind, warmth filled me. *Grandmother, I need your guidance,* I thought to myself. When I opened my eyes, there she stood.

"How can I help you, Grandson?" she asked, smiling.

That smile and her calling me her grandson did more to settle me than it should've. I told her all that'd happened since arriving in Scotland, and she listened without interruption, wavering in and out of sight.

After I'd finished, she sighed. "You need the people of Chemeketa. You should return there and seek their knowledge and guidance. You should also speak to your brothers. They are very wise, and so desperately want to know you. I've felt their longing since you left," she said.

"Really? But..."

"No buts. You are a part of them, David, and always have been. They are wonderful men with big hearts. Let them help you with your quest. Besides, they are supposed to." When I looked at her questioningly, she just chuckled. "Trust me, I'm not sure how or why, but this is as much a part of their story as it is yours."

I nodded, and sensing the link between us weakening, I thanked her and watched as she disappeared.

# Thirty-Four

## Muir

I watched as David left the Elders' beach and wished I could go with him. But I was part of the elite warriors of our community. If I left now, it would undo much of what David had accomplished today. So, I remained at my post, watching and listening as the crowd and the Elders discussed matters amongst themselves.

From what I could tell, it was close to a fifty-fifty split, half wanting to follow David's guidance—no surprise, it was mostly the young—and half arguing that they should take their chances here. To be honest, I thought fifty-fifty was good. I didn't expect the positives to be that high.

We were talking about uprooting ourselves from the only place we'd ever called home. A place we'd fought bloody battles with the Dorcha to hold. Now, not only were we being asked to leave but to do so *with* our enemies. I chuckled to myself at the absurdity of it all.

Once the crowd began to grow restless, the Elders dismissed us, and I immediately swam home to David. He was in his human form, leaning up against the back of the cliff wall, taking advantage of the evening sun. Even with the heatwave, the ocean was cold on human skin, and the breeze coming off it could be intense.

Assuming he was in his human form for a reason, I shed my pelt and walked up the beach to sit beside him. "You okay?" I asked.

"Yeah, as much as possible. How are you?"

"About the same. Relocating is a monumental decision for every Selkie, even if my place will always be by your side," I said, lacing my fingers with his.

He took a deep breath and squeezed my hand. "I'm going to leave for a while, go home to Oregon, and give you and your people time to discuss what's happened. I think they need to feel comfortable speaking freely without the Dion Adair hanging around."

I felt nervous about our being so far apart with everything so precarious. "I'm not sure that's a good idea. You're our Dion Adair, our protector. What if..."

He leaned over and kissed me. "There's no what if, Muir. I know you're safe here, at least for now. You may have to deal with some wayward tourists and the odd boat or ship, but those are things you're used to. But while I'm gone, I need you to do something. Something big," he said.

I looked at him dubiously. David never asked me for anything, so it felt awkward. "What is that?" I asked.

"I need you to meet with the Nuckelavee so you can be the emissary in my absence."

I stared at him like he'd lost his mind. "He'll destroy me, David. I don't have your powers."

"He won't if he wants to survive. I'm more powerful than him, and you'll be under my protection. Besides, if he wants to forge an alliance with the Selkie, he'll need an ally to make that happen."

I couldn't imagine meeting such a creature. I knew the Nuckelavee was over five hundred years old. He usually took the form of a Greenland shark, allowing him to prolong his life. Still, he'd spent many generations harassing and killing our people. Not just us, but humans as well. I just didn't trust him, no matter what David or his ancestors said.

"Will you do it?" he asked after I fell silent.

"Um, David, I-I don't know if I'm the right one for this job. I mean, I..."

"I understand you're afraid, Muir, but if the old man was right, the Dorcha are our only chance for survival. And I can't negotiate a treaty between the two. That must be done by a Selkie and a Dorcha, and obviously, I am neither."

I thought for a long moment. "This morning, when you mentioned it, you were thinking of me, weren't you?"

David nodded. "I've known since I met the Nuckelavee that you needed to be the one to discuss this with him. Why don't you speak with the Elders? If they agree, I'll introduce you and stay as an emissary while you get acquainted. I'll leave when you feel safe to continue the negotiations without me."

I agreed, both to appease David and because I couldn't think of another who would be willing to meet with the Nuckelavee in my place. That night, we were hit by a mother of a storm that seemed to reflect the attitudes of the entire Selkie population. Waves crashed on the shore, forcing most of us out of the surf to avoid injury. The storm was no less violent inside my own mind, since

I had no idea how I'd negotiate with the Nuckelavee. I was more than certain the Elders wouldn't want me to, but would follow David's advice. However, I was also obliged to follow their orders. It was part of my oath when I became a Selkie warrior. It seemed like I was stuck in an impossible situation. But then again, weren't we all?

By dawn, the storm had passed, and most of the Selkie settled in to rest. After we'd taken a long morning nap, David took off to find the Nuckelavee and talk to him. To my surprise, none of the Elders had objected to his idea of my meeting with the Dorcha leader.

As I lay on my beach, left alone with my thoughts, I felt the fear of what could happen engulf me. Nothing was scarier to a Selkie than a Dorcha and there were no Dorcha scarier than the Nuckelavee. What had I gotten myself into?

# Thirty-Five

## David

I KNEW I NEEDED to get out of the way and let the Selkie make their own decisions. Besides, if they decided to leave their homeland, I needed a plan for where to take them. For that, I needed help and expertise above and beyond my knowledge.

I met with the Nuckelavee after the council agreed to allow Muir to act as emissary. He broached no argument. "You must remember," I warned the Dorcha leader, "if you do anything to harm Muir, not only will you create an enemy of the very people you need as an ally, but I, personally, will declare war on you and all Dorcha. I'm putting my trust in you, and I expect you to comply."

At first, the Nuckelavee appeared stunned, then angry. I could tell he wasn't used to being challenged. I watched in silence as emotions warred across his face. The creature was intimidating at over seven feet tall, towering above me, and although the hatred that accompanied him when he first captured me was less, it was still there.

Ultimately, though, ensuring a future for his people won out. "I will do as you say. No harm will come to the Selkie warrior. How long will you be away?" he asked.

"I'm not sure, but I'll return when I have arrangements in place for moving the Selkie and Dorcha to safety. Until then, I'll try to maintain a connection with Muir and with you as well. Was it you who appeared in the form of a giant octopus on the bridge, trying to prevent my crossing?" The Nuckelavee nodded, not looking the slightest bit regretful. "Then you know where I'll be. If you need me, you can reach out to me there."

The images he sent me conveyed his agreement. I figured it was in good faith that I'd told him where I'd be. There was no reason not to. If I, or Dion Adair as they called me, couldn't force myself to trust the Dorcha, how would the Selkie?

When I arrived back at our beach, Muir stood in his human form waiting for me. "So, it is done?" he asked as I hauled out of the sea and removed my pelt.

"It is done, Muir. The Nuckelavee understands what's at risk. You must know that."

"I know we have been enemies for centuries. I know the creature has been personally responsible for the deaths of many of my ancestors."

"I understand, Muir. I really do. I wish there were another way."

Muir nodded. "So do I, but there isn't, is there?"

I shook my head. "No, I'm sorry."

Muir took a deep breath, letting it out slowly. "Okay, let's go."

After returning to Selkie form, we swam to where the Nuckelavee waited. I stayed back, watching, but not interfering while Muir met with the creature.

Images of past wars, offenses against the Selkie by the Nuckelavee himself, and stories of Dorcha misdeeds passed down over generations flowed out of Muir before he would even begin discussing anything.

The Nuckelavee bowed, not even trying to contradict Muir's accusations.

"So be it," Muir said. "We are not friends, but we can be allies." And the two began to discuss diplomatic strategies that Muir would take to his leaders.

When it was clear they were on common ground, I slipped away back to the beach and began packing for the journey home. All my belongings had been collected from my rented seaside cottage by one of the Selkie's friends, the small handful of humans who helped the Selkie youth who came out for their walkabouts. Apparently, these people were long ago descended from Selkie human pairings and through the decades were there to keep the Selkie youth safe.

Even though I hadn't used them since my arrival, I'd need clothes, money, and my phone to get back to Chemeketa and those who could help me figure out how best to deal with the crisis.

Muir met me just as the sun was going down. "So, you are leaving?" he asked.

I nodded. "In the morning. I'll need a day or two back in the human world to set up a return flight to Oregon."

"I will miss you," Muir said, as a rush of emotions surged through our connection.

I turned to him, knowing he could feel the same pain and sadness coursing through me. "How am I this attached to you in such a short time?" I asked when he stepped into my open arms.

He shook his head but didn't speak, just letting me hold him as we both prepared emotionally for our separation.

When he pulled back, he looked up at me with pleading eyes. "You will only stay away as long as you have to?"

I nodded. "I'll return soon, but hopefully in the meantime, you and the Dorcha will have planned how to nurture this new alliance between you."

"And if it doesn't work out?" Muir asked.

"It'll work out," I said. It had to. We both knew that if it didn't, disaster was sure to follow. If it did, well, that would give a reason to hope for a safe and harmonious future.

That night we lay in each other's arms, preferring our human forms because it allowed us closer contact. The next morning, Muir kissed me goodbye and left to meet with the Council of Elders. I dressed after he was gone, made the long trek to town, and caught a ferry back to the mainland.

Sadness engulfed me the further I traveled from our beach, not just because of leaving Muir, although that was mostly it, but also because I'd miss this wild place. I thought back to the time before I'd met Muir and how Oregon had felt as close to home as I'd ever experienced... Until now.

As the distance between me and the Selkie homeland grew, I realized why Ireland hadn't felt right and why Oregon hadn't been exactly right either. My heart belonged to the northern seas above Scotland.

I also felt how much of a sacrifice we were asking the Selkie to make in choosing to leave the area. The deep sorrow stayed with me as I flew back to the States. I only had the heart to text Marta that I was on my way back. She'd kindly agreed to keep an eye on my place while I was away, even though it was out of her way. She'd also offered to pick me up at the airport, but seeing as this was a busy time of year at her shop, I opted for a rental car.

When I arrived home, I crawled into bed and cried myself to sleep. I felt so alone, so lost without Muir. Home didn't feel like home any longer. I realized I was probably jumping the gun, but the following day, I packed my most precious belongings, put the boxes in the back of my car, and called the realtor who'd sold me my beloved cottage. "I'm ready to sell," I told him.

Of course, signing everything to get the place listed was easy. Giving up my solitary lifestyle was the hard part. But it felt right. I was asking for sacrifice from the Selkie and even the Dorcha, and I needed to do the same.

I grabbed my phone, opened up the group chat with my brothers, and sent them a text. *I'm back and heading to Chemeketa. I need some help making plans to move the Selkie to a safer place. Can you meet with me when I arrive?*

# Thirty-Six

## Muir

THE DEBATE BETWEEN THE Dorcha and the Selkie Elders was intense. Both sides had years of contention to throw at the other. Ultimately though, our fates rested in each other's hands. Somehow even the Dorcha seemed to understand that.

"When do you propose we leave? Where will we go? What place on Earth is safe now?" These were questions that floated around the council from Dorcha and Selkie alike.

Finally, after about a week of debate, with no solution in sight, the subject changed. "So..." Regani said at the beginning of a meeting with the Dorcha, "...how shall we integrate our peoples? I assume the Dion Adair will bring solutions when he returns, so our debates might be premature. What isn't premature is deciding how our two societies can get along well enough to work with one another."

The Nuckelavee stood silently with the Dorcha behind him. No one spoke while he considered the situation.

"Neither the Dorcha nor the Selkie will be happy about our collaboration. We have grown too far apart over the centuries. But you are right, we must make a change. If a delegation of Selkie agrees to come to the Dorcha stronghold, we can send some of our people to spend time with you here. By starting small, we can eventually integrate on a larger scale."

Regani glanced to the other Elders for confirmation, then nodded in agreement. "Nuckelavee give us today to choose our ambassadors, then we should meet again to discuss the integration." Regani said.

He left, taking the Dorcha with him. My heart beat fast against my ribs, as I knew I should be the one to lead the delegation. David had said as much before he'd left. As soon as the Dorcha were gone, I moved to the center of the chamber to address the Elders.

"The Dion Adair asked me to work with the Dorcha toward integration. Therefore, if the council sees fit, I volunteer to lead the group chosen to go to them."

Regani nodded her approval and the rest of the council agreed. Of course, my instinct was to gather only warriors. That would make the most sense considering the Dorcha had been our enemies since the Fae occupied this land. However, I knew such an approach would be seen as a sign of aggression and only lead to more conflict.

Not for the first time, I wished David was here to ask for advice. I drew in a deep breath, held it for a moment, and let it out slowly. There was no other way to accomplish what had to be done with the Dorcha. We had to move forward in good faith. We had to trust them.

I swam over to my parents' beach. "I need to have a serious conversation with you," I admitted and felt the bile rise in my throat as I pondered what I was about to ask—Aa sacrifice that could likely end in disaster and would be entirely upon my head.

# THIRTY-SEVEN

## DAVID

"How many Selkie and Dorcha are you talking about?" Lance asked.

I shrugged. "I'm sorry, I don't know the exact size of either population, but I would guess in the hundreds," I admitted. "That's assuming they all agree to relocation, though. When I left, they were still coming to terms with having to work together."

Lance shook his head. "You said you're a marine biologist. You know better than anyone what transferring such a huge group of aquatic animals into an existing ecosystem could do to it, not to mention magical half-human, half-seals, right?" he asked.

I nodded. "Yes, however, I'm not sure what the alternative is. They can't remain in their homeland much longer, they won't survive."

The Chemeketa leaders convened a council meeting as soon as I arrived in town. They listened as I explained the plight of the Selkie and Dorcha, but no one offered any real solutions. I'd blindly hoped I could bring both populations to the shores of Oregon to be protected by the people who respected the ways of magic. Being so caught up in the urgency of the situation, I hadn't considered the impact introducing new species would have on the environment. So much for my doctorate and concern for marine habitats.

Drew and Lance insisted that I stay at their place for as long as I'd be in Chemeketa. Lance said he and his brothers wanted to spend time with me, getting to know me, even if only for a short time. Remembering that our grandmother had said the same thing when I summoned her caused me to smile. "I'd like that too," I admitted.

That night, we sat around a campfire at the back of Drew and Lance's house. I was so anxious at the start, I could barely sit still, much less try to bond with the men. Things changed, however, when Kyle arrived. "Hey, I'm going to link with my boyfriend, Conley. I'd like you to meet him."

"The dragon?" I asked, and Kyle chuckled.

"Yes, sort of."

To my surprise and relief, a young man appeared instead of a fire-breathing dragon. I'd clearly not gotten over coming face-to-face with Kyle's terrifying dragon form months ago.

Kyle and Conley joined us around the fire, and the brothers and their partners tried to make small talk, asking about where I grew up and my stepfamily. I knew they wanted to know more about my relationship with our father.

I just couldn't concentrate on the brotherly bonding right now, though. My thoughts were consumed by all that was happening back in Scotland, and what should be happening here on my end. "I'm really sorry, guys. I know you all want to get to know me, and I want that too," I finally admitted when I thought I might crawl out of my skin. "But now might not be the best moment. I have so much on my mind."

I stood to go when Lance stood with me. "Wait, I know this is a lot, but I think we're all part of it somehow. If you'd be willing to discuss it with us, we might be able to help you."

Crea, the quietest of the group, added, "You don't have much to lose, do you?"

"No, I don't—" I conceded. "—and any suggestions are welcome."

I sat back down and explained the situation to them, just as I had earlier with the Chemeketa council.

Lance and Eli, Crea's partner, had heard it all earlier in the day, but the others hadn't. I wasn't sure how it would help, but hell, I'd take any ideas they were willing to give.

Finally, when I was done, the group sat silently staring at the fire. "You said you're moving the Selkie from Scotland, because it's no longer safe for them there, correct?" Conley asked. I nodded. "I-I don't live in your dimension," he continued. "I'm, well, Kyle and I now exist as a volcano in the in-between. A place we call *Dóiteán*.

"I know Avalon, the mythical place where the Fae settled, has integrated into that dimension as well. None of us have ever been there, because it's very secluded and isolated, but you could consider speaking with them. Maybe they will allow you to move the Selkie and Dorcha people there."

The mention of the Fae caused me to remember the night the ancestors came out of me and mentioned that the Selkie should seek the place where the Fae had gone. I guessed, I knew about the existence of other dimensions, at least theoretically, so Conley's revelations didn't come as a total shock. At this point, it felt like little actually could shock me. Still, I only vaguely understood what he was saying. "I'm not sure about dimensional travel or how to get to that dimension, let alone arrange convoys of people there. I'd need more information."

Conley studied me for a moment before he continued, "There are dimensional portals, like the one used to travel between *Dóiteán* and Chemeketa. You should come home with Kyle and me to speak with my parents and our spiritual leader Guha Cho. They may have insight for you on how it could work. Also, my father's people have a diplomatic relationship with Avalon. Maybe he would be able to advise you how best to approach them."

For the first time since all this started, I felt a spark of hope. Maybe, with the help of my brothers and their partners, I really could fulfill my ancestral destiny as protector of the Selkie.

***

I couldn't explain why my nerves were so frayed. It wasn't like I was asking for a million dollars. Instead, I was an emissary for a group of magical creatures seeking refuge. But as I stood watching the *Dóiteán* council scrying, as they called it, in a large opal basin, my heart was about to beat out of my chest.

Crossing through the dimensional portal, which appeared to be a hidden cave nature had cut into the coastal mountain, was uneventful. Besides a feeling of foreboding outside the cave, which Kyle had assured me were the ancestors of the air people who lived in the surrounding forest, and a gentle breeze as we walked through the portal, the passage had been easy. Unfortunately, it was also clear that the cave was too far inland for any of the Dorcha to cross.

Conley had been correct about his homeland. His father had been in contact with the leaders in Avalon, a place which, up until then, I had known only as legend. "They are very rigid," Conley's father explained. "They do not allow outsiders to come to Avalon, nor do they allow their citizens to leave and return. These people would be a threat to them, by definition. You must be very careful how you approach them and ask for permission."

Maybe that was why I was so nervous waiting for the *Dóiteán* council to finish.

Mr. Cho was the one who initiated the scrying, although, to be honest, it was more along the lines of calling someone on a phone.

Kyle and Conley stood on either side of me as the rest of the council chanted in the background when, after what seemed like forever, the water in the scrying bowl became opaque.

The water shimmered, and the face of a regal woman coalesced into being. "I am High Priestess Helena, and this is my council," she said, waving toward a group of people we couldn't see. "Why have you summoned us?"

Mr. Cho gave a slight bow. "High Priestess, we have come to you with a concern that requires expertise we do not possess. May we ask your aid and counsel?"

The high priestess looked annoyed. "We are here now, so you may proceed in making your concerns known, but understand if you have disturbed us for frivolous reasons, we will sever the connections we've allowed between our civilizations."

Mr. Cho hesitated and then lifted his hand to indicate to me. "This is Dr. David Franklyn, a witch from the Earth realm. He has been contacted by the great Selkie of the Scottish isles. I believe you may know that area as Scotia."

The high priestess's eyes registered shock as she turned her penetrating gaze on me. "You've been in touch with the Selkie?" she asked.

"Yes, and the Dorcha as well. Their future is in jeopardy, and I seek to help them find refuge from the dangers they face in this world."

Her expression changed from shock to anger. "How dare you..." she began.

Before I knew what was happening, an odd feeling came over me, not unlike the night we stood before the standing stones and my ancestors spoke to the Selkie through me.

"No, high priestess," I said in a voice that wasn't my own. "How dare *you* question me."

Several people around me gasped and to be honest, if I'd had control of my mouth, I probably would've done the same. The high priestess began to wave her hand, I assumed to shut down the communication, when a mist-like hand reached out of me, preventing her from doing so.

The old man who'd appeared at the sacred stones, one of my ancestors, stepped out of me and scowled into the scrying bowl. He lifted his arms, and said, *"And in the time of transition, will come to the priestesses of Avalon a message of the Selkie. And this time shall trigger the opening of the borders of Avalon once again, for the unification of the blood of the Fae shall be our salvation."*

The high priestess's expression morphed again, this time registering fear. "I-I didn't know, Chiad."

"Then, you are not qualified to be in your position," the man said with disdain. "Meet with your priestesses, tell them the prophecy has begun, then return to speak with David, for he will be the one you must work with to help the children of the sea make it to safety!"

The high priestess bowed, and the opaque water in the bowl turned clear once again.

The entire room stood speechless. "Great Merlin," Mr. Cho said.

The man laughed. "No, not quite," the wizard said. "I've been called that before, among other names bestowed upon me, but I lived long before Merlin's time."

"Why did she call you Chiad?" I asked like an idiot. I mean, why was I asking him anything?

He smiled. "David, I am the first half-human, half-Fae, as I told you before. My name is Gaelic for first."

I nodded, still feeling the intense power he radiated from when the High Priestess had been, well, hateful, I guessed you could say. I clamped my mouth shut, determined to lay low.

He continued smiling at me, clearly reading my mind. "Do not be afraid of me, David. I'm the same as the last two times we met. You have a long journey ahead of you, but I'm very pleased you have determined how best to help the people of the sea."

"Why didn't you just tell them we were coming?" I asked, once again surprised I had the audacity to question such a powerful wizard.

"Until you found the portal into *Dóiteán*, I couldn't be certain. My mother and I had predicted there would be a time the Selkie would come to ask the assistance of the people of Avalon, but I couldn't pinpoint the exact time. It only became clear when you crossed dimensions."

"Your mother?" I asked, getting confused.

"My mother, Queen of the northern Fae."

I remembered he'd told me that before, too, and nodded. "What now?" I asked.

"I will meet with the priestesses to determine how best to help you, then I will ask them to get back in touch. Mr. Cho, can someone maintain vigil over the scrying bowl?" he asked, and the spiritual leader, significantly paler now than he had been earlier, nodded.

"Yes, we will keep a vigil."

Chiad looked pleased. "Then I will take my leave. I'm sure the priestesses of Avalon are already gathered and waiting for me." With that, he disappeared in wisps of mist.

I closed my eyes and took a few deep breaths to gather myself, only to open my eyes to find the entire group staring at me.

I didn't know what to say. No words of wisdom or reassurance came to mind. I was just as overwhelmed as they were.

# Thirty-Eight

## Muir

Although weaker from the distance between us, my connection with David was still strong enough that I could feel his excitement. He'd somehow made headway. I wished I could return his positive feelings, but to be honest, I was on edge.

My father and mother had agreed to take our family to the Dorcha encampment. They'd decided going as a family demonstrated our willingness to consider a compromise. However, we were all afraid it would end poorly.

The meeting had gone fine. A Dorcha family had met us, which was good. At least it wasn't the Nuckelavee. That would've terrified my younger siblings.

The family had arrived in the form of harbor seals. They were smaller than us, which I assumed was the point since they were trying to look less formidable. The Dorcha still gave off a feeling of anger, though, so regardless of appearances, there was still mistrust that couldn't be put aside.

The Dorcha showed my family to a beach not far from the borders of the Selkie territory. When I was sure they were as safe as could be in this environment, I reached out to David, hoping he would be able to use his magic to more strongly connect us.

I ended up falling asleep, waiting for him to answer. As I slept, I began to dream.

*"David?" I asked, and noticed I was in my human form.*

*"Yes," he said before embracing me.*

*"Is this real?" I asked, snuggling into his arms.*

*"Yes. My brother, Kyle, and his partner helped me connect to you," he assured me.*

*I looked around and saw we were in a dark room, a huge white stone bowl filled with water its only notable feature. "Where are we?" I asked.*

*David chuckled. "I'm guarding that thing," he said and pointed at the bowl. "It's called a scrying bowl, and it's how we communicate with a high priestess from Avalon."*

*I shook my head, not sure what he was talking about. David regarded me for a moment, and seeing my confusion, said, "I think we may know how to save your people, and it involves working with the Fae in Avalon. We hope to create a place of safety for the Selkie to live like they used to, where you won't be in constant danger."*

*I nodded, hope filling me. Just then I heard a lot of noise coming from the sea, but it wasn't enough to pull me out of the dream state. David must've sensed my unease. "Muir, where are you?"*

*"Remember when you told me to work with the Nuckelavee to help build trust between the two communities?" I asked.*

*David nodded, concern on his face. "Well, my family and I are on an island just outside the Selkie boundaries. We are starting to bridge the gap between our two cultures."*

*"Wow, okay, and you took your family?"*

*I nodded. "Bringing my family here is the ultimate show of trust that they will not harm us. A Dorcha family has befriended us, and another family was sent to live among the Selkie. It is a true test of our ability to coexist in peace."*

*"Do you feel threatened?" David asked, his eyebrows drawn together in worry. I felt his loosened embrace of me tighten a bit.*

*I shook my head. "No, but they are so different from us. The Selkie are peaceful. We don't seek conflict and try to avoid it at all costs if we can. We use our powers to soothe those around us, whereas the Dorcha often do the exact opposite. They fight each other. They quarrel, they instigate. As a result, conflict surrounds us. It's nerve-wracking just to be around them," I admitted.*

*"Have you brought it up with the Nuckelavee?" David asked.*

*"No, this was our first day here. It's the first time we've encountered one another in this way, so we've only begun acclimating to it all."*

*David sighed and stared into the distance. "You'll have to speak with him and the council about your differences. If the Dorcha are found to be aggressive with the Selkie, that will disrupt this still fragile alliance."*

*"And if I push things too fast, that will as well."*

*David nodded. "What did your parents say?"*

*I laughed. "Not much, or my siblings. Mostly, they are terrified, same as me. But we all recognize the importance of what we're trying to do."*

*"Tell them how much I appreciate them taking this on," David said. "They should be remembered for their bravery and selflessness in taking this kind of step. I'll ask Chiad what he proposes next time I see him."*

*When I looked confused, David chuckled. "Do you remember the old man who came to us at the standing stones? One of my ancestors, the wizard? The high priestess from Avalon called him Chiad. That's much easier to pronounce than the name he gave us, wouldn't you agree?"*

*"Yes, I remember," Chuckling at the truth of what he'd said about his name. "He showed us images of past magical creatures using the stones."*

*"He's helping me communicate with the priestesses in Avalon. Apparently, there is a prophecy that one day the Selkie will come to the priestesses for help, and Chiad is ensuring they understand that time is now."*

*I gazed into David's ocean-blue eyes for a long time before I sighed. "I hope this will work out, David, because so many things are working against us. Our relationship with the Dorcha, convincing everyone to leave their homeland... it's all so confusing and difficult."*

*"I know," David said and brought his hand up to gently stroke the side of my face. The feeling of him touching me again, skin to skin, began to heal broken parts of my heart I hadn't even known were there. "When will I see you again, David? I miss you."*

*David smiled at me before leaning down for a deep kiss. "You're seeing me now, but soon. As soon as I know what to do, when our plan is in place, I'll come to you."*

*Just then, the water in the white bowl behind David began to shimmer. He turned as the clear water turned milky white, then a woman's face appeared.*

*"The priestesses have met, David Franklyn, and we will accept our responsibility to help the sea people in their time of need."*

*When the woman in the bowl turned to me, her eyes widened. "You are Selkie?" she asked, sounding surprised by my presence, and I nodded.*

*"Then, it's true. Of course, it's true. Chiad wouldn't have come had it not been. But forgive me, I've never seen a Selkie with my own eyes, just heard legends."*

*"It is my pleasure to meet you. I am Muir Fen, Selkie of the Scottish isles," I said, unsure what else to say.*

*She bowed her head. "The pleasure is mine. On behalf of the priestesses of Avalon, this is an honor. Let us speak now of what must happen to save your people."*

# THIRTY-NINE

## DAVID

F EELING MUIR WRAPPED FIRMLY in my arms once again only steeled my resolve to see this quest through to the end. I was surprised and pleased that the high priestess had contacted us while in our dream state. I guessed  I was living in a constant dream state of sorts, though, being in a dimension between the veil and the Earth realm.

*"We've debated and worked with Chiad, and yet we are still unable to determine a manner in which to build a portal to Avalon. When we closed the gate between Earth and the veil, we secured it in such a way that would prevent anyone from entering until the time of rejoining."*

*"Which is now, correct?"* I asked. *"Isn't that what Chiad said?"*

*The high priestess shook her head. "The beginning of the prophecy says the boundaries will begin to break down, and we will once again join the world, but that isn't something that will happen quickly. And many things must be done before that will come to fruition.*

*Meanwhile, Chiad said the sea people were in grave danger, therefore, we will do what we can to assist you."*

*"So," I said, feeling hope slipping away, "what must we do?"*

*"A portal exists there, does it not?" she asked.*

*"Yes, though it isn't anywhere near the land of the Selkie, and inland travel will be difficult if not impossible for the Dorcha. But you believe they will have to come through here?" She nodded. "Then, what happens? How do you propose they pass from Dóiteán to Avalon?" I asked.*

*Her face held worry. "Avalon's borders can't be breached. People can leave our world, but they cannot return. For now, the land destined for the Selkie is not directly linked with Dóiteán. However..." she said, and paused a moment as if in thought, "...the arrival of the sea people in Dóiteán will begin a process of undoing our boundaries. In time, the sea people will be able to complete the journey to their new homeland."*

*"And the sea in Dóiteán, is it safe for them?"*

*She looked perplexed. "We only have access to a small portion of our oceans. We do not think they are different from your own, but you must ask the inhabitants of Dóiteán what they know, for they will have a better understanding than we do."*

*With that, the high priestess became distracted as someone began talking to her. "I'm sorry, I must go now. David, Muir, we will do what we can to help. I apologize for what I said to you before. The prophecy is ancient, and being the high priestess when it began to come to pass was a shock."*

*When her face vanished from the scrying bowl, I turned back to Muir, still with me in the dream state.*

*"So, it begins. I'll remain here a few days and speak with people in Dóiteán to learn what I can of the oceans here. I'll try to reach out to you again when I have more information."*

*Muir looked sad, and now that the business side of things was over, I pressed my lips to his again. "It's okay, my love," I said. "Things are working out, okay?"*

He nodded, and just like that, the dream ended, and I was alone in the chamber with the great scrying bowl still and silent beside me.

# FORTY

## MUIR

I FELT BOTH REASSURED and anxious after the dream with David. I knew it had been real, having been there and meeting the great priestess. I also remembered the news about Avalon, the would-be homeland we wouldn't be able to reach even if we ventured through the portal David mentioned.

The Nuckelavee met me the next morning as I prepared to swim away from where my family was staying. "I have news from the Dion Adair," I said. "I need to go to the Council of Elders and share what I've learned."

The Nuckelavee regarded me for several moments before he said, "I would tell you to share it with me now, but I can see that to do so would be a breach of the trust you've placed in our alliance. I will accompany you to the council."

"And will my family be safe here?" I asked, not even trying to be diplomatic.

He nodded. "We will not harm your family, as they are under my protection, just as the Dorcha who are now within your borders are safe, no?" he asked.

"They are safe from us, Nuckelavee, but the Selkie are not prone to violence. I have not noticed the same from the Dorcha."

Again, the great beast regarded me, before responding, "The Selkie and the Dorcha are different, but we are not prone to violence, as you say. We may be more aggressive than you, but that comes from generations of living on the edge."

He looked out over the great expanse before us, then said without looking at me, "When the Selkie were afforded certain protections, the Dorcha had to survive on our own. At first, we were able to keep humans away by scaring them. Sometimes we attacked them to prevent them from..." He shook his head. "Life has been difficult for the Dorcha, Selkie. You see a people who are violent, whereas I know them to be people determined to survive by any means necessary."

"But—" I challenged, "—you were always violent, even before humans took to the seas. You have had little tolerance for them or us."

"This is true, at least in part. Mostly, we were angry with the Selkie for excluding us, but then generations passed, and my people began to forget. I am the last of the Dorcha from that time. Even trying to teach them the old ways had little lasting impact. Their collective anger subsided, and they began to settle into the oceans peacefully. We became allies with the Mer people. We even had loose relationships with witches who communed with water, but then humans began to take to the oceans, killing us at will. We waged war against them for as long as possible, but they continued to come at us. What you see today is a broken people."

I sighed next to the great creature, feeling empathy for him for the first time. "We've been blessed, Nuckelavee, we know that, but there's much water between us that must be crossed before our people can unite. Will the Dorcha be able to calm themselves among the Selkie? If not, I fear the Selkie will reject unifying our two societies."

He looked out over the water in silence for several moments, considering. "If you can teach us how, I think they will try. But we can't be the only ones to change, Selkie. Your people must make an effort as well."

I nodded in agreement, then went to inform my parents I was leaving for the Elders' beach. They seemed fine, even at peace, swimming with the Dorcha family still in harbor-seal form, discussing the decrease in salmon, a favorite lament of the Selkie.

Clearly, the Dorcha family were also upset about that, and I felt relief they had found common ground.

I swam with the Nuckelavee to the Elders' beach and was pleased to see the council convened. As we came out of the water, I heard one of the Elders speaking positively about the Dorcha family who'd arrived on our shores.

"I have news," I said when the council acknowledged us.

I explained the dream and the involvement of the high priestess in Avalon. When I mentioned her, the Nuckelavee's expression grew grim.

I thought for a moment he would respond, but when he didn't, I resolved to ask why later. After giving my report, including how well my family was doing living among the Dorcha, I swam back toward the Dorcha stronghold with the Nuckelavee. "Why didn't you like it when I mentioned the high priestess?" I asked as soon as we were alone.

He didn't respond for several moments as we swam. Finally, he sent images of a meeting held many years earlier between the Avalon priestesses of old and the Dorcha. I saw as they pleaded with the priestesses to help them gain a foothold among the magical people.

They were rejected, the reason being they'd been cursed by the Great Fae Queen. "I'm the only one left who remembers the meeting," the Nuckelavee said. "However, their rejection still stings."

"Do you trust the priestesses?" I asked. "At least enough to accept their advice about crossing into their dimension?"

"In the past, I wouldn't have, no. However, if they can help us guide my people to a place where the Dorcha and Selkie are free from the dangers of human overpopulation, then yes, I will trust them. I must do what is best for all Dorcha, regardless of any personal misgivings."

"Then, so be it," I said. "We will continue to work with them to find a way to secure our futures."

# FORTY-ONE

## DAVID

I MET WITH THE high priestess several times over the following weeks. She gave us as much direction as possible, even sharing research on expanding our portal to bridge the gap between the land and the sea, so the Dorcha could cross it without being transported on land.

Muir and I connected several more times through dreams, and each time he seemed more optimistic and excited. One night, he was ecstatic. "The Nuckelavee has connected with the Mer people." His jubilant mood subsided some, as he continued, "There are less than a thousand of them left. Most live in remote areas, terrified of humans. But those who remain wish to join us, David. They are eager to cross into the new dimension."

"Are there other magical sea creatures that would want to come too?" I asked, and Muir shook his head.

"No, there are only a few such populations remaining, the others are now extinct."

That statement was enough to sober us both. Unfortunately, that same reality was in store for the Dorcha and Selkie if we didn't succeed.

When I was convinced I had gleaned as much information as possible from the Avalon priestesses, I met with Mr. Cho, my brother Kyle and his partner, Conley, and a few others in *Dóiteán* about building a bridge portal between the ocean and the existing cave portal.

"We don't want this portal to be permanent," Mr. Bolcan, Conley's father, said. "It would be dangerous to have two portals open to our community, and we aren't prepared to keep two secure for any length of time."

"We can't know when Avalon will be accessible to them until it is," I explained, "They may need to return to this realm, or for others to cross into it."

"Then, it needs to be a portal that can be closed unless it's needed," Mr. Cho said.

I nodded, and when I looked at Mr. Bolcan, I could tell he was surrendering to the idea. "What is it that we need again?" Mr. Bolcan asked.

Kyle had assured me that although our grandmother was weaker now than when he and our brothers had faced our father's cantation, she could help create the bridge to the sea.

There was also a need for a personal sacrifice, something that would enhance the magic and create the portal. The price of establishing the original portal had been the loss of Conley's ancestor's ability to return to the Earth realm.

This time, the one to pay that price might be me. I was pretty sure I wasn't ready to make that commitment. However, in my heart, I also knew if it came down to it, I would make that sacrifice for Muir and his people. Even for the Dorcha, victims of humanity's selfishness and oppression.

I put that little piece of information aside for now. More pressing matters were at hand, like determining exactly how to get the sea people, as the high priestess called them, from their rocky Scottish isles to Chemeketa, and doing so with humans being none the wiser.

# Forty-Two

## Muir

D AVID AND I LAY in each other's arms in one of our shared dream states.

*"So, tell me about your trip from Scotland to Oregon, leading up to when I found you in the cave," David said.*

*I shrugged. "It was dangerous. I had to avoid storms and great ships, and got lost several times despite possessing the Dion Adair's stone to help guide me."*

*"Do you think the Selkie can navigate the same waters you crossed?"*

*I shook my head. "No, I don't believe they can. It would be treacherous even for my fellow warriors, let alone families with children, but I will ask the Nuckelavee and see if he has an alternate path we can follow."*

*"Really? It sounds as if you have developed at least a working relationship with him. That's good."*

*"I have come to understand him and the Dorcha more than I thought possible, but we are still struggling with bridging our differences."*

*"Keep trying," David said, giving me a supportive squeeze.*

*After the conversation died down, I just relished being in David's arms. I was so thankful for the dream states. Time when I could be with him and feel him next to me.*

*It was strange to be with him like that, though. Strange, in a way that made my pelt itch. It wasn't natural for me to dream so vividly. Honestly, I didn't think I'd ever remembered a dream before. Now, I recalled every moment spent with David in this blending of dreams and reality.*

The next day, I mentioned the travel dilemma to the Nuckelavee, and he looked pained. "Yes, we have been discussing that as well. I'm afraid you will not like the route we recommend."

"Why?" I asked, feeling concerned.

"It is quite hazardous, and even we don't have control over some of the creatures we will encounter on the trip."

When I looked at him, confused, he added, "We think we should follow the Northern Sea Route."

I still didn't know what he was referring to until he sent images of polar bears attacking Dorcha as they attempted to cross the sea route. He also flashed me images of ice forming over open sea, locking creatures into areas where they drowned or were trapped and were once again vulnerable to the bears.

"Is there no better way?" I asked.

He showed me the route I had taken, and I knew it was fraught with even more dangers than the one up north. "We will have to go that way then," I confirmed.

"And that means we must leave soon, before winter sets in."

That information was alarming. Were the Selkie ready to leave? I wasn't sure, but the discussion needed to happen now. So, the Nuckelavee and I appeared before the Council of Elders again and shared his ideas with them. That night, I told David, and he looked as dismayed as I felt.

*"That sounds precarious," he said. "Are you sure there's no other way?"*

*"The Nuckelavee said it's our best chance. There is no safe route, only a potentially safer option."*

*David thought for a long while before responding. "In that case, you must be prepared to leave by the next full moon. That's your best chance of getting through before the pack ice settles in. Can you mobilize by then?"*

*I shrugged. "Not without you," I admitted.*

*David's lips brushed mine then, and I could feel the love and encouragement he poured into the kiss. "Okay, I'll return to Scotland but, Muir, you need to have the Selkie, Dorcha, and the Mer people, if they're coming with you, ready to leave by the time I arrive."*

*"I'll do what I can."* I said, and then snuggled into him for comfort. Something I really needed a lot of at the moment.

# FORTY-THREE

## DAVID

I BEGAN RESEARCHING SHIPPING routes as soon as I returned to Chemeketa. There were two options to consider. The Northern Sea Route, which wound go through the north past Russia, then down the Inside Passage from Alaska to the Oregon coast, or the Northwest Passage through Canada.

The Nuckelavee had warned that polar bears might be a problem. Unlike sea creatures, they were less persuaded by our abilities to soothe and repel adversaries, so if they came across one, they would most likely attack.

There weren't vast numbers of polar bears who would stand in our way, but according to the Dorcha, the ones who would be waiting for us were starving. "The power of persuasion is lost on creatures struggling to survive themselves. We will be seen as food rather than a passing curiosity," Muir had reported him saying.

When Muir presented the Nuckelavee with my alternate idea of the Northwest Passage, he'd explained we were safer facing the boats along the Northern Sea Route, following the Russian coastline. I knew the Nuckelavee spent most of his life in the Arctic Ocean and he knew the shipping routes better than anyone, so I had to trust him. In the end, we did.

*"That's a lot of trust we're putting in the Dorcha," Muir pointed out the night we both agreed to support the Nuckelavee's proposed route.*

*"We don't really have any other viable options. He has to know if we don't get the Selkie safely to Oregon's coast, the Dorcha won't have much chance of getting through either."*

*"I just wish I had a way to know for sure that this will work," Muir admitted.*

*"I wish I had a way of making sure myself. I'll be with you, though. I've decided to make the journey too, and if anything goes awry, I can help."*

That night, after I woke up, I lay in bed thinking about everything these people were being asked to do. Trusting their most bitter enemies with their lives, with nothing but their good faith and my ancestors' warnings to go by. It was a scary proposition with no guarantee of success.

I ended up catching the same private jet back to Scotland, and the pilot said he would help transport any sick or elderly Selkie via plane. It was a kind offer, but watching Muir struggle in flying across the Atlantic, I was almost sure none of them would accept. Of course, we'd have to see, so I thanked the pilot and told him I'd let the folks in Chemeketa know of our final plans.

By the time I reached the Orkneys, I felt exhausted and dirty from the travel. All I wanted was to bathe, see Muir, and sleep. I decided to forgo a hotel and had a taxi drive me to the beach. I slipped my foot into the water and waited for Muir to connect with me. Connect and hopefully meet me with my pelt so I could join him, letting the sea refresh me, build my energy reserves back up, and then sleep cuddled up with my man.

# Forty-Four

## Muir

I FELT DAVID'S ARRIVAL on our shores, and knowing I'd have him back in my arms soon made me happier than I'd been in a long time. With that joy came a rush of sadness, though, because his presence meant I'd be leaving my home within a matter of days.

I shed my pelt upon reaching the beach and the moment David saw me, he ran into my arms. "I've missed you so much," he said as he held me tightly and pressed kisses along my neck while breathing in my scent.

"I've missed you too. I brought your pelt. I want to swim with you."

David smiled, stripped, and stashed his clothes, then donned his pelt as I did mine. As we swam among the kelp beds, he sent images of his trip, time he'd spent with his brothers, and the new dimension in the in-between, as he called it. I knew it was to fill me in on what he'd accomplished, and while I was proud of him, it was the furthest thing from my mind right now. I only wanted to spend time with him, to revel in his closeness, before our responsibilities caught up with us.

Finally, he seemed to get the message, and we played in the water, diving and leaping from the surface, just living in the happiness of us as a couple.

Exhaustion eventually took over, and I should've known David would be fatigued by his journey. Even the thought of flying on that horrible machine again tired me.

That night we lay wrapped in each other's arms in a sea cave, much like the night he found and saved me. Our first time making love. Strangers, but somehow not.

But that was all the time we were given to spend together, just the two of us. The next morning, I felt the Nuckelavee waiting outside the cave entrance and went out to greet him.

"I can sense the Dion Adair is nearby. Is he here?"

I was just about to say he was asleep when David came out behind me, also wearing his pelt. "I'm here, Nuckelavee."

It was almost as if the creature sighed with relief when he saw him. "That is good, for I'm afraid there are more dangers than anticipated."

David's look of confusion matched my own. Then the Nuckelavee sent images of Russian ships gathering in force off their coast. "I believe it will be safer if we go through the Northwest Passage, even if it means facing more polar bears."

The Nuckelavee hesitated, then added, "If we don't go now, we will be forced to contend with more ice, making the bears even more dangerous." He looked at me. "You should speak to your council, for if we can't leave within the next week or so, we should wait until the spring thaw."

David nodded. "I agree, damn," he said, then turned to me. "Can you prepare the council? I should speak to the Nuckelavee in more detail before we discuss this with the Elders."

I nodded and rushed toward the Elders' beach. It was still early, so I knew they wouldn't be there yet, but the main guards would send scouts to fetch each councilmember when I informed them the Dion Adair had called a meeting.

Once the great chamber filled with the Elders, David and the Nuckelavee arrived to discuss the new threat and change of plans.

I was impressed at how patient the Nuckelavee was as he answered the council's questions. He explained how the pack ice grew and of its dangers, as well as that of the polar bears.

The Council of Elders was clearly alarmed, and understandably so. "I said this to Muir, and I'll say the same to you. If we cannot leave within the week, we should wait until the spring thaw. Our best chance of success requires we go without further delay," the Nuckelavee concluded.

"We aren't ready," Regani said, and I could tell she was about to call off the move.

"Then those who aren't ready will have to stay back," David said. "I'm sorry, Regani, but it's more dangerous to hold off. The boundary protections are now completely down. The Selkie have had numerous close calls this summer, and I assume they were close rather than fatal only because of my predecessor's momentary strengthening of the boundaries. If we don't go now, there will be casualties, of that I'm sure."

He waited a moment, then added, "Anyone who wishes to join us must be ready to leave in three nights."

Regani looked ready to argue, but Caelan caught her eye, and she paused. "I understand, Dion Adair. We will let everyone know to prepare for the journey."

We spent the rest of the day helping prepare the Selkie to leave their homeland. Anyone who couldn't or didn't want to travel the distance by sea could travel via the flying machine, David had told them. To my surprise, several agreed, but I was sure they had no idea what they were up against.

When I spoke to David about it, he told me he'd reach out to Chemeketa and ask if they could send people to help keep the Selkie calm during the flight, just as Marta had done for me. Ultimately, Caelan and Regani agreed to lead those who wished to travel by air instead of swimming.

"I'm actually quite glad they're doing this," David told me. "I haven't spent time in the oceans of *Dóiteán*. It's a great opportunity for the Selkie people to get the lay of the land, well, sea, before we bring in the other sea folk."

The discussion about searching the new oceans was what persuaded Caelan and Regani to do so. Of course, when they agreed to do it, most of the council's Elders decided they would fly as well.

It would be better for them physically, too, since Caelan and Regani were quite a bit older, as were most of the councilmembers. Caelan pulled me aside after that decision had been made, and said, "You will speak for me on this journey, and fully reclaim your place as head warrior," he said. "I know you are close to the Dion

Adair. You will be working as a team, and the people will follow you as long as you both agree."

Regani came up behind him and agreed. "The first key to leadership is to argue in private, then present a united front. Nothing scares people more than thinking you are not prepared to keep them safe."

I bowed my agreement and then spent time preparing them for air travel. "It's not my first time," Caelan said, surprising me. He chuckled at my expression. "When I was doing my *coisich mun cuairth*, I met several land humans my age who took me up in their plane."

"And you are willing to go again?" I asked.

He laughed out loud. "I enjoyed it once the thrill of being in the sky settled. It was beautiful and peaceful, like when you're in the sea, with no other creatures around."

I nodded, thinking that might be a good analogy. However, I had been so afraid on my trip that I hadn't had time to feel that sort of peace, even with Marta's soothing chants.

Selkie don't have possessions, not like land humans do, so preparing to leave was more about coming to terms with it emotionally than anything else. The only thing I carried was the sapphire necklace against my throat, the Dion Adair's stone, as I had the first time. The power that it once held had gone, but it felt like a good luck charm, and because David wore the sapphire bracelet his grandmother had left him, it showed a united front to my people.

Those making the journey by sea were ready to leave by the end of the third day, just as David had instructed—physically ready, at least. Emotions ran high and feelings of sadness and anxiety, even fear, were palpable among the group.

Those making the journey by air had left on the big flying machine the day before, and along the way Regani had collected David's possessions from where he'd stashed them on the beach. No Selkie had chosen to stay in the ancestral land, and there was a collective feeling of melancholy about what we were leaving behind. Even the gathered Dorcha were showing signs of stress about the trip.

David and the Nuckelavee swam out first, with the highest-ranking Dorcha and Selkie warriors, me included, following behind.

A coalition of warriors from the Dorcha and Selkie swam behind the lead group, while the rest either flanked our large traveling pod or brought up the rear. We would also be stopping in Iceland to collect the small Mer tribe that would swim with us through the Northwest Passage. The Nuckelavee had said they were familiar with it, so they would also be our guides.

We were on our way. Sorrow was heavy in us all as the Selkie sent images to one another of the places along our ancestral grounds they loved the most. Sea caves, sun-warmed beaches, patches of ocean where the currents flowed through and brought abundant swarms of tasty fish, now passing into the realm of memory. It was the end of an era, and although we all felt some excitement for the journey ahead, we were also mourning all that we would never have again.

# FORTY-FIVE

## DAVID

THE JOURNEY TO THE Arctic Circle was, thankfully, uneventful. We traveled from the Scottish isles to the Faroe Islands on the first day, which was a long journey, although it was still part of the original Selkie territory. The Dorcha and Selkie alike were tired after the long swim across open water, so we took a break before continuing on to Iceland.

"I'm very glad we sent our young, elderly, and infirm on the flying machine," Muir said.

I nodded. "Yes, I was concerned about how well they'd do on such a long journey."

"It'll get better once we reach Canada," the Nuckelavee said, surprising us. He'd turned himself into a gigantic Greenland shark the moment we got to the Faroe Islands and had all but disappeared from view. Neither of us knew he'd transformed back into his usual intimidating self.

"But that's when we have to watch for polar bears," I said, causing him to nod and flash feelings of concern at us.

"As long as we are careful, I think we will be fine," he said. "The bears will be looking for things to eat inland at this time of year since there is almost no ice,"

"Unless they swim out to meet us," I said warily. I wasn't an expert on polar bears, but I did know they were expert swimmers, and I also knew seal was a favorite prey.

We spent several nights traveling around Iceland, and that was when I began to enjoy the marine elements of our trip. It wasn't until a pod of narwhals with a beluga adoptee swam among us that I realized I was letting my fears keep me from embracing this new experience. The Dorcha were also becoming friendlier, and even they seemed to be taking the time to enjoy this epic journey we had undertaken together.

That night, I noticed my calmer demeanor was helping Muir as well. I felt bad knowing his nerves were frayed, because I was giving off such tense energy. *That's it*, I thought. *I'm going to be much more Selkie-like from now on.*

I knew before we started that seals could stay out at sea for several days, so our long journey didn't concern me in that way. However, the northern seas were known for bad storms. Each day before we ventured too far, I'd cast out my senses, using the air energy I acquired from the Chemeketa people, to see if any storms loomed and then navigate our way around the worst of them.

There were days of rough weather and choppy seas, which concerned me, but neither the Selkie nor the Dorcha seemed in the least bit worried. They were all much more experienced swimmers than me, after all.

When we finally arrived at the tip of Greenland, I sensed something distinct but unfamiliar in the water around us. Something I couldn't identify. I was just about to put everyone on high alert when the Nuckelavee, in his shark form, angled sharply toward a pod of sea creatures swimming toward me.

They felt different from sea mammals and fish, and that was when it occurred to me. These were the Mer people. The Selkie began to move their ranks toward the shore, which was the only place we'd seen in a while not covered in ice. The Dorcha never went on land, so they scattered to find food. I stayed with Muir and a few other warriors and waited for the Mer people to reach us.

I had no idea what to expect as the creatures drew closer. They didn't look anything like the merfolk of legend or modern pop culture. Long legs were fused and ended in flipper-like feet with no scales. They had a humanoid appearance but looked more sea mammal than human. I imagined if they were seen off the side of a ship, people would assume they were dolphins or whales of some kind.

Images swam through my mind as the group greeted us, but like the first time I'd met the Dorcha, I couldn't decipher what was being said. I looked to Muir and clearly, he didn't understand them either.

The Nuckelavee ended up being the interpreter. "These are the Mer people of the North Atlantic," he said. "They wish you well."

I returned a similar greeting, then asked him why we couldn't understand each other.

"Because they have yet to bite you."

"What?" I asked in alarm. "I have to be bitten to understand them?"

I felt ambivalence flow through the Nuckelavee. "Most things in the ocean bite. It isn't always meant as an act of aggression," he sent back.

A large male came closer, his bright blue eyes taking me in. I put my flipper out as a greeting, and flinched as he bit me, barely puncturing the skin. "Greetings, landling," he said, and I could hear mirth in his comment.

"Greetings to you," I sent back, unsure what to call him.

The meeting wasn't as auspicious as I figured it would be. Of course, as I spent time with them, I understood it would've been quite different had we not been announced. They were extremely wary of anyone not totally of the sea. "Under normal circumstances, we'd even be wary of the Selkie," the male who had bitten me said. When they explained this to us, I got the feeling they were friendly with the Inuit people, but that was just a glimmer that came to me. Their language, a mix of images and what sounded like whale calls, was still so odd that I wasn't catching everything that was said.

That night, the Mer people, who incidentally weren't opposed to that name, explained that they had settled in Greenland in the summers for safety. They would often travel with pods of whales to warmer climates during the winter months, but they had to be careful to avoid being detected.

When the leader of the tribe, Enki, came on land and transformed into a godlike man with dark skin, bright blue eyes, and a chiseled body, I almost fell over. When I looked at Muir, he was giving me a very jealous glare.

Still being in my seal form, I sent him an image that I hoped meant, "What do you expect? He's gorgeous."

Muir ended up chuckling, which was a relief. Then we both took off our pelts and greeted the man. "I didn't know you could transform," I said.

Enki smiled. "Only for a short time, then our skin dries out and we suffer. Unlike you, we can only be out of the water for brief periods."

I noticed he was still sending mental images to me, so I asked if he could speak. To answer my question, he opened his mouth, and a loud screech came out that sounded like an animal in distress.

"That's a no, then," I said, and Enki sent an image laced with his strange-sounding song that basically equaled a chuckle.

"We are not of humans like you, the Selkie, and the Dorcha. We are of the ancient Fae. We are of the sea."

"That explains why you can't leave it."

He nodded, then moved back into the surf, and transformed into the sea mammal from before.

"We will need assistance moving across the land, if that is what you have in store for us," Enki shared.

"I don't think that will be necessary. We're working with witches to build a portal to cross into another dimension. The portal will be connected to the sea in this realm as well as the other."

Enki sent images of the Mer people doing magic. The message was that they could help. That was good to know. "How well do you do with polar bears?" I sent back.

He flinched. "No creature does well with the majestic white bears," he replied. "We must use caution, and maybe you can use your magic to fend them off." He hesitated. "I have friends, they are of the Inuit people and have power over the white bear. But they dislike Ijiraq."

He sent me an image of the Nuckelavee in his current shark form, then images of him in his scary form, but instead of being part horse, he was part caribou. He was kidnapping Inuit children and leaving them abandoned.

"That was centuries ago," the Nuckelavee said defensively.

"Yet they don't forget," Enki sent back.

Although we were communicating in images, the thoughts of the Nuckelavee were almost like he was muttering under his breath, and it was something along the lines of "I said I was sorry."

The exchange would've made me laugh, but I remembered the stories of the Nuckelavee in Scotland. Terrifying cautionary tales that, as it turned out, were all likely true. I could imagine he was just as horrible to the people here, and if they'd been traumatized enough to name him, I could certainly see why they wouldn't trust him now.

"If the Inuit can help us stay safe, we should reach out to them."

I looked over at the Nuckelavee, who appeared to be pouting, and said, "Tell them if they help us, we will remove the Ijiraq from their lands forever."

The Nuckelavee shot me a nasty look, which this time did make me laugh, and before long, he chuckled as well. "That's probably the best way to convince them to help," he finally agreed.

Enki met with his friends–Inuit priests who still practiced the ancient ways–and returned to report that they would help cloak us using magic, hiding us from the white bear and the Inuit people. "They will not understand what you are doing and are likely to hunt you more than the bears," Enki said, relaying what the priests had told him.

"Will they disguise the Dorcha as well?" I asked.

Enki shrugged. "As long as the Ijiraq isn't involved," he said, indicating the Nuckelavee, "I'm sure they will."

I looked at the Nuckelavee, who nodded his agreement, and when the priests came to exert their shamanic powers, he disappeared until after they left.

Before departing, a regal-looking woman who seemed to be in charge of the priests admonished, "This is just a smokescreen. You must be vigilant, and you must move through the pass quickly. Travel at night when our people are less likely to be hunting, and you must place the Qalupalik along the edges of the group to ensure our magic doesn't diminish as quickly along your journey."

"Qalupalik?" I asked later after the Inuit priests had gone, and Enki sent an image of himself and his people. "That's what the Inuit call us."

"And you are accused of taking children too," the Nuckelavee said, still clearly miffed about the conversation.

"But ours is just a legend to keep humans, children especially, away from us, which helps protect all Mer people. You really did kidnap their children."

"True, but I left them where their families would find them."

Enki, clearly still amused at what must be an ongoing argument between them, let the subject drop, but not before giving the Nuckelavee a side glance.

The next day, we swam through the heavy currents between Greenland and North America. According to Enki, we were lucky to be going through now, because as the temperatures dropped, the current became even more difficult to swim against.

It wasn't a swift current, but we were happy to see land again after passing through the strait. Just as we were about to go ashore, three enormous whales surfaced in front of us. *Bowhead whales,* I thought to myself, surprised at how big they were.

Enki swam up to them, and after what seemed to be a long conversation, he returned to us. "We have been granted passage," he said, then swam off without an explanation.

Were the whales guardians of this area? I would have to find out later, if possible. I was just thankful that, other than the Nuckelavee, the Dorcha all chose to take the form of harbor seals to better blend with us on this journey. Had the bowheads seen a massive pod of orcas, a natural predator, swimming their way, I doubt our passage would've been granted as easily.

That night, I was relieved to have the shore to sleep on and Muir to snuggle with, even if it was intensely cold. I was more than happy to have my pelt to keep me warm, as I was sure if I were in my human form, I wouldn't survive for long in these elements.

I didn't see Enki that night or the day after, which we chose to use for a nice long rest before we braved the last perilous stretch of the Northwest Passage.

The day we left, I swam ahead with the Nuckelavee, and the three bowhead whales showed up again. Muir came up behind me, and we waited as Enki swam out to greet them again.

"We are to follow them. They have offered to show us the quickest route through and enhance the Inuit priests' magic."

When Enki swam back to us, I questioned him. "Why are they helping us?"

He sent an image of whaling ships harpooning them, leaving blood-stained oceans behind. "They understand why we are retreating from our homelands," he said before swimming back to the rest of the group to relay the message.

We only saw one of the much-warned-of polar bears, but he was not paying any attention to us. The lack of danger from that direction left the entire migrating pod the time and leisure to experience this new land. It was incredible, first flatlands and then distant mountain ramparts that rose like a wall against the world. The bowhead whale guides stopped each day when we came across beaches they felt were safe for us. Of course, I also cast my senses out to detect any predators or humans we needed to avoid.

I found it relaxing, if not meditative, watching the whales feed after we broke ranks. They were amazing creatures, and huge, at least double the size of the humpbacks or gray whales I was used to seeing from a distance on my whale-watching tours back in Oregon.

Several weeks passed before we finally reached the northwestern shores of Canada and the end of the Northwest Passage. The bowheads warned Enki the waters would get rougher as we went into the Bering Strait, and we would need to stay close to shore as we moved south.

I met with the Selkie warriors and began to discuss tactics for avoiding boats and human interaction. I'd warned them that once we passed through the Arctic Circle, we'd be dealing with a lot of human activity again.

Of course, I was prepared as well. The magic the Inuit priests had used to conceal us was similar to a spell cast by the original Dion Adair. There were elements of it that were different, and I didn't quite grasp them all, but I believed I could use my own powers to replicate it. I had to at least try to create the same type of smokescreen to hide our progress as we moved south, down the western shores of Alaska and Canada and then into Washington and Oregon.

I told Muir about my plan to use the spell, and he seemed pleased. "You should ask for help, David. I know you are powerful, but the Mer people are as well. You no longer have to depend only on yourself."

He was right, of course, and I made a point to speak with Enki the night the bowhead whales took their leave. We were in much more dangerous waters now on many levels. It was time to become even more vigilant as the Dion Adair, the protector of our people.

# Forty-Six

## Muir

As we moved down the coast of what David referred to as Alaska, I was overcome by its intense beauty. I almost suggested we settle there, but for the presence of the polar bears.

As we swam, the human population began to grow again. Still, nothing like we were used to in our old territory, but David assured me that would change as we went further south.

"You should look for areas where you feel the Selkie would be safe, in case the Council of Elders determines that *Dóiteán* isn't appropriate," David advised as we entered the waters of what he said was Canada.

It was also beautiful, still wild and rugged like Alaska, and another potential home if we had to remain in this dimension. There were plenty of sea caves and secluded beaches for us to take refuge. Of course, there were also a lot of seals already occupying the area, and I wasn't sure how much our presence would disrupt them.

We were a relatively small group, no more than a few thousand strong, but that many seals in one place could completely disrupt the ecosystem. We were not that kind of species. We wanted to enhance nature, not cause harm.

I made a note to ask David about it in case the dimensional shift didn't work or go well in the long-term.

When we passed Washington and reached the coast of Oregon, I noticed the population and water pollution was worse than in Scotland. There was no way we could live here and not be in more danger than before. The fishing had also grown increasingly slim since leaving Alaska, so when we finally came ashore near Chemeketa, we were hungry and exhausted.

Fortunately, the Chemeketa people had prepared for our arrival. They had cast barrier spells to protect us from other land humans. They also greeted us with much-needed food, bringing cases of fresh fish to the beach to feed us.

The Dorcha, some of whom had been to this area before, broke off after assuring David they would check in periodically, and went further out to sea to fish and recuperate. Meanwhile, David met with Chemeketa's leaders about creating the portal into *Dóiteán's* oceans.

That was where things began to divert from the plan. Regani and Caelan met us three nights after we arrived off Chemeketa's shore. "The oceans there are good, suitable for the Selkie and Dorcha," Regani assured us. "But the portal between the worlds is proving more difficult to create. Several attempts have been made by the *Dóiteán* and Chemeketa leaders working together, none successful."

I listened as they discussed with David the challenges they'd encountered. Magic, or witch energy, had diluted in the generations since the portal was created.

Even combining the Dion Adair's magic with that of the *Dóiteán* and Chemeketa witches wouldn't generate enough power to create a new portal.

The Selkie and maybe even the Mer people could transform into their human form to travel across land to reach the existing portal, but I wasn't sure how the Dorcha would manage. Of course, that was a major decision, not one to be made lightly. "We should speak to the Nuckelavee and get his opinion," I said. "This affects them more than the rest of us, and it's crucial they know we are there for them. We can't leave them behind."

David looked at me strangely, but nodded. Later that night, I asked him about it. "You seem to have changed your position on the Dorcha," he said. "I know we've made progress, but..."

I rolled over to look at him. We were sleeping in his brother's home in Chemeketa, so we were in human form. "David, we have made huge strides improving the relationships between the Dorcha and Selkie that hadn't been bridged in centuries. They are our cousins, we are of the same people. I can't abide the thought that we would betray them now."

David nodded. "Nor shall we, even if we have to put them in water tanks and transport them by truck to the forest and into the portal, that's what we'll do."

"That's only right," I said and turned back over, confused why David would be so surprised. There were few things more important than your word, and the Dorcha had done what they said they would, now we must do everything in our power to ensure they arrived safely in the new lands too.

# FORTY-SEVEN

## DAVID

I HADN'T MEANT TO upset Muir. I wasn't implying the Selkie should desert the Dorcha, it was just that I was surprised his attitude toward them had changed so much.

That was a good thing, and even though I knew he was upset with me, it made me feel hopeful about where we were as a group. The next day, I again met with several leaders of *Dóiteán* and Chemeketa, which included my brother, Lance, and his partner, Drew, about the portal.

We tried several things, tapping into the different elemental powers and casting ancient spells, but nothing seemed to work. Worse, the more we tried, the more darkness settled around the area. When I mentioned it to the group, Lance sighed. "Yes, that's the last of what we believe to be our father's cantation."

"Why is it showing up now?" I asked, staring at the grayish fog that hung over the ocean.

"Because, you're the one who will end the curse once and for all," Drew answered.

"So, not only are we working on relocating or expanding the portal, but we're also dealing with the curse?" I asked.

Both men nodded. "If it helps, this probably means the solution to the portal is somehow related to ending the curse," Drew added.

I took a deep breath and let it out slowly, frustration filling me more and more. "Okay, then how the hell do we end the curse?" I asked.

Lance and Drew made eye contact, then looking over at me, Lance said, "We should probably connect with Kyle and Conley, and maybe we can get Crea and Eli to join us. I think we need to summon our grandmother and get her opinion, and perhaps her help."

I nodded. "Well, there's no time to waste. I'll let the party know what's happening, but if you think our grandmother can help, we should try tomorrow."

After Lance and Drew agreed and our meeting ended, I went down to the beach and found Muir in seal form. I quickly slipped on my pelt and joined him, gesturing toward the sea.

He happily joined me as we swam through the tall kelp forests lining the shores. Finally, I encouraged him to swim to an ancient sea stack. When we arrived, I climbed onto the tiny ledge just big enough for Muir and me to sit on, glad none of the other creatures in our party had claimed the spot for the night.

As soon as we were nestled together on the rock, I told him what Lance, Drew, and I had discussed. "It seems my birth father might be part of the reason we can't get the portal to work. We're going to summon my grandmother for direction on how to break the curse once and for all."

"And with the curse lifted, you can open the new portal?" Muir asked.

"That's the theory."

"What do you think?" he asked.

"I don't know," I admitted. "I mean, I didn't know my birth dad that well, and I certainly didn't know I had brothers or anything about my grandmother."

"Can it hurt to try?"

I stared out at the water for a long time while Muir sat patiently by my side. Finally, my thoughts were clear enough to express why I was struggling. "I came to Oregon for school and the sea, but mostly to find my birth father. He and I were never close, and he and Mom split up when I was still very young, but at least he was a connection. My stepfamily wasn't that supportive after Mom died, and my stepdad started seeing someone else shortly after."

I paused, letting myself remember the pain of rejection, knowing I had to face it if I were to face what came next in the journey.

"When I couldn't find him, I decided I was better off without family. I decided if it hurt that much to be rejected, I was lucky to be alone. I guess by contacting my grandmother, and letting her and my brothers help me, this will all become real." When Muir didn't react, I sighed. "It's easier accepting I'm in love with a Selkie than to accept I have family that might want to be a part of my life. Does that make sense?"

Muir slipped his pelt off and sat on the rock, his warm brown eyes wide and staring at me. "You're in love with me?" he finally asked.

I chuckled as I slipped my pelt off too. "Yeah, I'm in love with you. I have been, I think, since that first night in the sea cave. Nobody, human or Selkie, has ever meant what you do to me."

Muir smiled and crawled into my arms. "I'm in love with you too. I'd like to be your mate, if that's something you'd like."

"It is, Muir. Let's make it official. Will you be my husband?"

Muir's smile grew before he kissed me deeply. "Mate, husband, whatever you want to call it, I'm yours."

We lay in each other's arms that night, stretched out on our rocky perch. I cast a spell to keep us warm, so we could remain in our human forms. Muir fell asleep quickly, but I lay awake listening to the waves as the tide came in around us. What would it mean to have a family again? Would they reject me like my stepfamily had, or embrace me as I'd once hoped my birth father would someday? Could I trust them with my heart as I did Muir?

I felt Muir move against me and I couldn't help but smile. Trust, that was what all this came down to. I hadn't known Muir much longer than I'd known my newly found brothers. Yet, I trusted him with my life and my heart.

Nothing Lance, Crea, or Kyle had done made me think they would reject me. Even if they did, I was a grown man, able to care for myself. I was not that same young man, barely out of college, needing help to get through graduate school, and still reeling from the death of his mother.

I remembered how Mom had supported me, and even how my stepdad and stepsiblings had backed down when she got onto them about their expectations that I should follow the same career path they'd taken. Like going into marine biology was majoring in underwater basketweaving or something. It was almost funny now to think how in the past year, I'd used my degree in ways I could never have imagined.

I still missed my mother. I missed family. Even though it hadn't been perfect, and my stepfamily had made it clear I was no longer welcome in their lives. I missed having people, missed belonging.

I thought of the Selkie, of Muir and his parents and siblings. Even of the Dorcha and Mer people. They were all connected, all family, however distant. Maybe it was time I accepted the possibility that, yes, I could let go of my fear of attachment to Muir. Perhaps I even had enough strength to let go of my fear of connecting with my brothers and even our ghostly grandmother.

It was time to open my heart and let people back in, even if it did scare the crap out of me. That was what was needed to break the curse, and that was what I needed to feel whole.

# FORTY-EIGHT

## MUIR

HEARING DAVID ADMIT THAT he loved me unleashed pure happiness. I'd already decided I loved him and wanted to be his life mate, even though he wasn't Selkie, and I'd never be able to be away from the sea for too long.

In the story of David's ancestors, the witch who fell in love with a Selkie, they'd intentionally lived on land. Ultimately, the Selkie had sacrificed his pelt and life to be with his wife. I supposed I could do that, but I didn't want to lose my connection with the sea. If David truly loved me, as he said, then he must love and accept that part of me as well.

Luckily, David was a sea creature himself, even before he was truly aware of it, even down to his choice of scholarly study, and learning to interact with the inhabitants of the sea before he became one of them. We would have to discuss his expectations, but I had to hope he'd be willing, at least to a large extent, to create a life with me in the water.

The next morning, I woke to David already in his pelt, searching for fish or crabs. I quickly joined him, and we hunted together in harmony, swimming around one another and laughing as we lost breakfast more than once, because of David's silly antics.

We swam back to the protected beach, and hauled out to where we'd stashed our clothes just in time to see Drew walking toward us, so we quickly shed our pelts and dressed. "I'm glad you're back. I spoke to the family, and they all said they could get away by lunch. So, I propose we eat here, then go over to *Dóiteán*."

"Do you know how to contact our grandmother? I mean, I have this..." David said, pointing to his bracelet, "...but I'm guessing it's just for me."

Drew nodded. "Yes, that's a connection between you and Gwen only. Your brothers and I discussed it. We think you should summon her on the shore of *Dóiteán*, which means once we cross the portal, we will still have a day's journey to get there."

David took my hand and drew me toward town as Drew followed alongside us. "We'll let the community know what's happening. I'm guessing several Selkie will want to go with us. Is that okay?" David asked, and Drew nodded.

"I think that'll be fine. The Selkie council is already established there, and the Elders may want to join us too."

The entire trip over proved stressful. In my time with David, I had grown more accustomed to being in human form, so I did better than most out of the water. But even I was fatigued by the long journey, hiking up the mountain into the forest to reach the cave portal, then venturing through it.

By the time we arrived in the town of *Dóiteán*, I was exhausted. The food offered to us was not what we were used to, so most of us ended up fasting that night, which wasn't that unusual. Seals only ate when they found food. As the fish stocks around our former homeland had thinned over time, there were nights when we didn't eat.

The following day, we all got up early and began the journey to the sea. It took a while before we reached the coast, but hope and excitement overrode any lingering fatigue and hunger. The *Dóiteán* ocean glistened, its deep blue water beckoning me, and towering sea stacks lined the shore much like the Chemeketa coastline. We were greeted immediately by the Council of Elders, who seemed pleased to see us.

Regani and Caelan met me after I slipped on my pelt and moved into the water, ready to be off the land for a moment.

"How was your journey?" Regani asked.

I nuzzled beside her, indicating I was happy to see her again, and pulled back. "It was tiring, almost worse than riding in that flying machine."

Caelan chuckled, and I knew he wasn't in agreement. Based on experience, I was convinced few things were as bad as a Selkie traveling by air.

I spent the evening asking them questions about this area, our temporary if not permanent new home. Was there enough fish to sustain us, the Dorcha, and Mer people? What was the underwater terrain like? Were there dangers we hadn't anticipated?

Regani glanced at Caelan before responding to any of my questions. "It's paradise," she finally said. "The sea life here have no idea what to think of us, so getting acquainted will be an adjustment, but we've encountered an abundance of creatures that disappeared from Earth long ago."

"Do you think they'll welcome us?" I asked.

Caelan smiled. "Not even the largest of sharks, which are bigger than the great whites in the Earth realm, have shown any interest in us other than curiosity. We don't appear to have any natural predators here and there are no humans to contend with either, at least not in this part of the ocean."

"It's good then?" I asked.

Both Caelan and Regani nodded. "We haven't seen anything that would make us think otherwise."

"Have you encountered any magical creatures?" I asked, curious if there were others like us here.

Both shook their heads. "We are the only ones, I think," Regani said.

"Why didn't our people migrate here when the portal was created?" I asked.

I knew neither of them knew the answer, but I still felt compelled to ask. Considering everything we'd gone through since humanity had begun to impede our way of life, I did have to wonder why we weren't brought into *Dóiteán* when the Fae crossed over.

As our conversation turned back to more pressing matters, I explained about the planned ceremony with the Dion Adair and his family to summon David's departed grandmother. "David asked if the Elders can be present when he does it, in case your counsel is needed."

"We'll let them know," Caelan said.

Before they swam away, Regani turned to me. "You did well, Muir. You have helped our people discover a new world in which we can grow and prosper. As challenging as it is to leave our beloved Scottish isles behind, I am confident we can establish a new home here."

I nodded, but didn't tell them the prophecy Chiad had told us. Access to Avalon remained blocked, but our arrival in *Dóiteán* would begin the removal of their walls. That seemed like a whole other challenge to address and not one that should interfere with the issues at hand.

This world was going to be so different from our homeland. For several centuries, Selkie territory had encompassed a relatively small area. We now had an entire ocean to explore, and we'd already been on an intense journey. Our Elders, young, and infirm had flown through the skies. The rest braved unknown waters, facing threats of polar bears and humans alike. I knew our legends would be ripe with the stories for centuries.

I could only imagine the adventures yet to come. And adventure was the way to think about it. This dimension's oceans were open to us. Given our new alliance with the Dorcha, perhaps we could partner with them and the Mer people to create expeditions to explore and learn more about this world. Not to mention the fact that we were told by the old wizard that we would need to make an effort to embrace our human side and befriend the people of *Dóiteán*, who had already done so much to help us.

I guessed what encouraged me the most was, this world was reportedly full of people descended from the Fae. We weren't likely to face humanity that wanted to destroy us, either deliberately or by disregarding the health of our shared environment.

That was worth more to me than anything else. Our people, the Dorcha, and Mer people all living together in harmony and free from the dangers of our former home. Perhaps that's what the Fates had destined for us all along.

# FORTY-NINE

## DAVID

WITH KYLE AND CONLEY'S help, we gathered the groups in both dimensions, one group in Chemeketa and the other in *Dóiteán*, before casting the spell to call my grandmother forth.

For some reason, it felt important that all the magical sea creatures were gathered together, even if across the dimensions, like something inside was telling me it would be an auspicious moment.

As the moon began to rise over the horizon, my brothers and I stepped barefoot into the ocean, and they began to chant around me. Shortly after, the sea creatures started chanting in unison, and when I took Muir's hand in mine, a giant tsunami began to form and roll toward us.

We weren't in our seal pelts, and my brothers were at risk too. As the wave grew, I shouted, "What the hell!" With Muir's hand still in mine, I thrust my hands into the air toward it.

The towering wave stopped, as if frozen in place, although I now felt the menacing presence within it. "What is that?" I asked as the wave loomed over us.

"Dear old dad," Kyle said, nerves making him sound out of breath. "I'm guessing only you and Muir can cast it away, David. You must act together, as we did with our partners when facing his cantation."

I closed my eyes, lowering my hands as Muir tightened his grip, and sending as much energy into the wave as possible. It immediately fell away, only splashing us slightly as it disappeared back into the surf.

"Grandmother," Lance said, "we call on you tonight. If you can hear us, we ask that you join us on this beach."

The chanting around me had continued even while the tsunami threatened to envelop us. From where the giant wave had once been, a blue light formed and began moving toward us.

As it drew closer, I began to make out the image of an older woman. When she finally arrived onshore, she came directly to me. "We meet again, Grandson."

Tears filled her eyes, and I saw real regret there. "I will mourn never getting to know you in life as my grandson, young David," she said. "You know, David was your grandfather's name. Your father loved him very much, so I'm not surprised he named you after him."

She looked over at the others and smiled. "I've missed you all so much," she said and went down the line of my brothers before returning to stand before Muir and me.

"I've been able to follow you on some of your journey from Scotland to here. Although I was never strong enough to make myself known, I know what you are trying to do."

She turned then and, raising her hands, called out to where the wave had been.

*"With darkness no more, I reclaim this wave, and ask that it come with a portal to make."*

Thunder rolled, sending an electrical charge through us, and the wave rose again.

When she turned back, the light around her glowed brighter, her features looking younger than they had just a moment before. "David, seed of my soul, do you love Muir, creature of the sea?"

Not sure where this was going, all I could do was nod before finding my voice. "Yes, I love him."

"Muir, do you love David?" she asked then.

"Yes," he said without hesitation.

"Would you pronounce your love and commit to one another in front of your family and your people?" she asked.

"Yes," we both said at the same time, and I smiled as I heard cheering all around us.

"Do you have the sapphires?"

As Muir gripped the stone that hung around his neck, I held up my wrist and the bracelet I'd been wearing since I became the Dion Adair.

*"Spin and move, up and down, let these be a symbol now.*

*With their love proclaimed to be, with their hearts they call the sea."*

My grandmother's light became brighter, lighting up the beach like it was daytime. I felt the darkness around us, a darkness that'd been with me my entire life that I hadn't recognized until now.

*"Banished forever the curse from my seed, my grandsons are freed from the hatred of thee."*

Lightning flashed around us, and the air smelled of ozone.

*"Now that the world is once again cleansed, we open a portal from one world to another."*

"Put your pelts on and swim into the wave," she commanded.

Both of us nodded and quickly did as she instructed, swimming side by side as fast as we could toward the huge wave that hung motionless just offshore. The other wave had been created with malice and ill intent. This one just towered in place, waiting.

When we arrived at the base of the wave, my grandmother made it known she was there with us. Her energy infused it, and I knew it was safe. "Swim up, swim all the way to the top. Declare your love to one another once you are there, and I'll do the rest."

I nodded and paused momentarily, looking at the woman, who now appeared to be my age or younger. She smiled at me sadly, and I feared this would be the last time I saw her, at least the last time in *Dóiteán*.

Muir nudged me, and together we began to swim up the great wave. It was hard, gravity pulled us down as it should've been pulling the wave down, but we fought our way up, up, up until we reached the top.

I didn't dare look down. Not that I was afraid of heights, but I had to admit being atop a massive wave conjured by magic was terrifying. I could hear the chanting that hadn't stopped, I could feel my grandmother's presence, and it was almost more than I could handle. Nothing about it made sense, other than having Muir by my side.

When I turned to my love to say something to that effect, I saw him. Truly saw him, as if I were laying eyes on him for the first time. All the sacrifices he'd made. His love for his people, and now for the Dorcha and Mer people. And his love for me.

"I love you, Muir," I said, without even thinking about what my grandmother had told us to say.

I could feel his happiness through our connection, and the emotions he cast at me told me in every way possible, he felt the same.

I turned back toward my grandmother just as she burst into a bright blue light and vanished from sight.

That light grew around us, and a cold, intense burning erupted from my flipper where the sapphire bracelet was under my skin. I looked at Muir, and the sapphire stone he wore under his pelt was also glowing. Within seconds, the blue light narrowed into two shafts of light that embedded into each of our sapphires.

The wave slowly disintegrated, lowering us back into the sea and its calm water. As Muir and I began slowly swimming toward shore, I looked at my mate, who I loved more than any other, and saw a glowing blue sapphire tattoo at the base of his neck.

He sent an image of me telling me I had one as well, on my flipper. I didn't have time to think much about it, though, because where the wave had been moments before, the water began to swirl. In a matter of moments, one by one, Dorcha, Mer people, and Selkie emerged from the whirlpool, a newly formed portal into *Dóiteán*.

Once they were all through, our glowing tattoos began to fade and disappear from view.

"We did it," I said as Muir swam around me. "We really did it."

I left him to get reacquainted with his people... *our* people, while I continued toward shore. I felt compelled to do so. I shed my pelt and walked up the beach to thank the six men I now considered family. My brothers and their partners, who also had glowing tattoos that were beginning to fade.

"This was it?" I asked. "The end of the curse our father created?" All six of them nodded, a mixture of relief, joy, and exhaustion on their faces. "And our grandmother?"

"Sacrificed herself to end the curse and open your portal," Drew said.

"Did you know she turned back into a young woman before she passed over?" I asked.

Drew smiled, but shook his head. "No, I only saw the same dear friend I've known and loved all these years."

"I think she was happy to go, if that makes it any better."

"It does," Drew said, wiping a tear away. Lance wrapped his arms around him and kissed his temple.

"I need to stay here and celebrate the success of our quest, but I'd like to visit you before all this is over," I said, looking at the men in front of me.

"There's plenty of time," Lance said, Drew still snuggled into his embrace. "We would all like that."

"Hey, next month, *Dóiteán* is holding a big celebration for Samhain," Conley said. "I can see if the townspeople would be willing to do that here, on the beach, so we can all formally welcome and get to know our new residents."

"That sounds good, although I'm guessing a lot of people may be out exploring the ocean, but I'll be here, and maybe Muir will join us as well."

"Muir is a yes," he said, coming up behind me and slipping his hand in mine. He was followed by Regani in her human form, while the Nuckelavee, still in shark form, loitered in the nearby surf.

"The Council of Elders will join in the festivities as well," Regani said, then began shaking hands with my newly found family.

"The Dorcha will as well," I heard the Nuckelavee say and was surprised to realize I could now understand him while in my human form.

I translated his agreement to the group, then smiled. "It appears we'll be having a beach party," I said, and the group laughed.

"Before you go," Regani said, "On behalf of all Selkie and our cousins, we appreciate all you and the Chemeketa people did for us."

"It will never be forgotten," the Nuckelavee added. "You are and will always be welcome in our seas."

I doubted my brothers, or their significant others, understood just how much that meant coming from a Dorcha. Even witches weren't something the Dorcha tolerated before, so to hear the Nuckelavee extend that olive branch meant a lot had changed.

That night, blue light continued to bob through the waters, and the following day, the Nuckelavee said all curses on sea folk had been lifted. Several Dorcha had come ashore with him, showing us that for the first time in generations, they were able to leave the sea.

"Really?" Muir asked, eyes wide. "It must've broken last night when we opened ourselves to your witch brothers."

"You all, Selkie and Dorcha alike, let go of the hate you once harbored too," I said. "That's what fueled the curse that held my brothers and me back. My father's hatred. Now that you've released your mutual hatred of your cousins, and of the land humans who made your former homeland unsafe, you've been given back your own humanity."

"Last night was auspicious," the Nuckelavee said, "...and now I can rest."

I didn't know what that meant until a week later when we met with the Dorcha to begin discussing exploring the areas around the cove. The Nuckelavee had begun aging rapidly and told us that his time on this side of the veil was finally over.

"When the Great Fae Queen cursed us, I was forced to remain here to see, as she said, 'the consequences of my hatred.' That was more than twenty-five centuries ago. I've watched my people attack humans, then watched as humans hunted them. But until now, I didn't know what the Great Fae Queen meant." He smiled at us, seeming more at peace than I'd ever sensed from him. "This will be the last time I will see you, so thank you for showing me what I wasn't able to learn before now. Most importantly, thank you, Dion Adair and Muir Fen, for gifting me your friendship even when it seemed an impossibility."

I hugged the large, strange creature, who no longer felt like a monster to me. "I'll miss you," I admitted, and he smiled again.

"Like your grandmother, I'll still be with you. Something tells me, like her, our journey together isn't over, even though we will have both crossed the veil."

I didn't know how to respond to that, surprised at the lump that had formed in my throat, so I just nodded and didn't try to stem the tears that slipped down my face as the Dorcha leader swam with his people out into the clear, cold waters of our new home.

# Fifty

## Epilogue: David

### One Month Later

"Beware," Conley warned, then laughed. "Samhain is very different here than in your dimension."

"What he means is, the ghosts here are thicker than the people," Kyle added.

When I continued to look perplexed, Kyle chuckled. "We are a bridge between the living world and the veil into death. When the veil weakens on that side, it fills on this one. You can hang out with, talk to, even touch ghosts from that side of the veil."

"Um, scary," I said, making both Kyle and Conley laugh again.

"No, not really. It's more like a party here because the dead are not unlike the living. It's basically like a big family reunion across several generations."

"And there's no mischievousness?"

"Oh, there is, but it's all lighthearted and the living are just as responsible as the dead. The really nasty folks aren't allowed to come through the veil, so that's not a problem."

I was spending the night at Conley's parents, as we were all preparing for the party that would bring the sea folk together with the *Dóiteán* people. Muir had stayed back since there was still so much to be done to prepare for life in this new world.

So far, everything had been amazing. I was serving my year in Chemeketa, as I had agreed to prior to my quest, to learn the ways of the magic the people there had gifted me. Drew and Lance kindly let me stay with them in our grandmother's old home, and my best friend Marta visited often. But, I also spent copious amounts of time in this dimension with Muir, the Selkie people, and the other sea folk.

Sometimes Muir would join me in Chemeketa, but only for short stints since he wasn't comfortable remaining in human form for long periods. I'd already begun scoping out a spot above the *Dóiteán* shoreline where we could call home. Although, as yet, that hadn't been an issue. I loved spending time in the sea with my beloved mate.

Being a part of this transition between worlds was truly remarkable, although it wasn't without some challenges. For one, encountering the ancient sea creatures living here took some getting used to. The first time I faced a megalodon, I thought I'd crap myself, but the vast monster didn't show the slightest bit of interest. Not only did we possess soothing Selkie powers, but we were likely just too small for it to bother with.

Great whites were its favorite meal, and several of the Dorcha that favored taking that form had to rethink their shape. Here, it was likely a megalodon would attack first and think about it later.

Not that the Dorcha only stayed in the sea. As had been foretold by my ancestors, the sea folk freely interacted with our new *Dóiteán* neighbors both inland and along the coastline.

The night of the Samhain celebration, the townspeople, Conley and Kyle in their dragon forms, along with the three famed dragons of *Dóiteán*, showed up at the beach.

The people of Chemeketa had also agreed to cross the portal to celebrate Samhain and the arrival of the magical sea creatures, so they, too, were mingling with Selkie, Mer people, and Dorcha. I enjoyed introducing Marta to so many of the Selkie I had come to consider friends as well.

As Conley and Kyle had said, ghosts were everywhere. Most of them ignored us, and I hadn't seen anyone I recognized. Between all of the land and sea creatures, humans, and ghosts milling around together, it looked like the normally quiet beach had transformed into a busy waterfront metropolis.

Eventually, I ended up hanging out with Muir, my brothers, and their partners. I also met Lance's daughter Jennie–*surprise, I apparently have a niece*–along with her girlfriend, we all gathered as a group on the spot I'd chosen for a new house. Kyle whipped up a bonfire and we formed a circle around it, all bundled up in blankets and sleeping bags my brothers had brought.

We grew quiet when our grandmother's blue light began to glow in the distance. I sat up and pointed it out to my brothers, and by the time she arrived, we were all sitting up waiting.

"Hello, my family," our grandmother said as she landed among us.

I hung back as my brothers, niece, and Drew greeted her. After she came over to me and Muir and hugged us, telling us how proud she was things had turned out the way they had, she stepped back. "I'm not alone, boys," she said to the group. "Would you let your father speak to you tonight?"

Lance spoke first. "Grandma, is he dead?"

She nodded. "Yes, he crossed the veil less than a week ago. When the cantation no longer had control over him, he was able to die in peace."

I watched as the three men who'd become my family looked at one another, then at me. "David?" Lance asked.

I shrugged, my indifference warring with the feeling I'd never truly gotten closure. What my brothers had gone through, growing up amid intolerance and living with the curse, seemed much worse than what I'd experienced with an absentee father. He'd abandoned me, but I'd never been close to him anyway. How could you miss someone you never really knew? Of course, now I knew that was also part of the curse, the one my brothers had cast against him.

The man I hadn't seen in years and only recognized from a few photographs stepped into our grandmother's light. Seeing him now, in the flesh, I definitely shared many of his features. My eyes looked almost exactly like his, as did my nose, which my brothers had versions of too. There was no denying I was the man's son.

I watched as he entered the circle and stood before my brothers. "I-I can't ever apologize enough for what the three..." He paused, looked over at me, and sighed. "I mean, the four of you went through because of me."

"Why?" Crea asked as we all stared at the spirit of our father.

He glanced back at our grandmother, then turned to us. "It's hard to explain, but when I lost my father..." he said, directing his gaze at me, "...the man I named you after, I was lost." His eyes lingered on mine for a moment before he looked back at my brothers, and continued, "I let your mother's family convince me our lives, the ways of my people, were evil, and I needed to renounce them."

"So, you cursed us, because you couldn't stand up to your in-laws?" Lance spat out, bitterness in his voice.

"No," our father said, shaking his head. "I mean, yes, I never stood up to them. My primary duty should've been to love and protect my children, and I failed you all. But the curse was a mistake, Lance. When I hit you and you spilled blood, the curse was cast. I never knew how to reverse it, and it only continued growing stronger with time."

"You could've tried, at least," Kyle said.

"I did try, but I was so caught up in my own self-hatred, I didn't seek outside help like I should've. Not from your grandmother, or the people of Chemeketa. I shut that world out completely," He looked at me guiltily. "I'm sorry, David, for shutting you out, too."

"You never told me or Mom that I had brothers. I had a family and you kept them from me. Did she know you were married? Why did you have a baby with her if you had no intention of raising me? Did you feel even a little bit sorry for leaving me behind?" I asked, and could feel the bile rise in my throat. A lifetime of questions, all the pent-up resentment and hurt, came pouring out of me.

The man stood there and took it all, looking pained but resigned, as if he'd expected the onslaught. "We met on a business trip. I'd taken off my wedding ring, all part of my self-loathing and resenting my wife's family, and your mother was none the wiser. We maintained a long-distance relationship for years... I was living a double life of sorts."

I glanced at my brothers, who were slack-jawed in complete shock at the revelation. So much for the pious churchgoer they'd believed our father had been. He took a deep breath, as if reliving the past hurt him too, then continued. "Your mother was such a good woman and wanted a baby so badly that I couldn't deny her. I visited often, but when it became clear you'd both be better off without me in your lives, I stopped. I desperately hoped you'd be free from the curse, but I was wrong. Your mother never knew anything about it. I regret all of it but you, David. I'll never be sorry for having you as my son."

I had to force myself to resist the bitterness, sorrow, and loss that swept through me. "I forgive you," I said, then turned back to where Muir was still sitting. For all of his regrets and apologies, in life and now in death, my father was lost to me. He had given me nothing but heartache... well, that wasn't entirely true, he gave me three men who I had already come to accept as my family. My brothers.

When I looked over at them, I saw a similar resolve on their faces. Finally, after an awkward silence, our grandmother stepped forward. "I'm taking your father across the veil tonight, and he will have many years to heal the rift he created in his soul. If any of you have anything else to say to him, you should do so now."

I was not sure what came over me, but feeling a sudden sense of urgency, as if my ancestors—our ancestors—were compelling me to speak, I turned to him. "You made a lot of mistakes, and I don't think of you as a father, not really. I don't think I ever have, but you did bring me into the world and brought me together with these men, and they are my family. A family I never had before. Thank you for that, and may you find peace through the veil."

My brothers were smiling at me, and before long, they began to speak with one another and our grandmother. At some point, our father faded from view. It was strange to see him go, and my heart was now devoid of any anger or frustration, replaced with only love and respect for my new family.

Seeing the same emotions reflected on my brothers' faces confirmed it. Even after everything our father had done to them—to me—he was the past. The future lay in those gathered around me here in *Dóiteán*. My brothers, niece, their partners, Marta, the sea folk gathered on the beach below, and, of course, my mate. As if reading my thoughts, which he practically could through our connection, Muir stood and wrapped his arms around me in a firm, loving hold.

I didn't know whether or when the prophecy would be fully realized, and the sea folk permitted to enter Avalon, or if they would even want to go there when the time came. For now, we were safe, happy, and embracing our new life here. My shared quest with Muir was over, but our life together was only just beginning.

Flex inherits his family's ranch and begins being plagued
by prophetic dreams. Will his love for motel owner
Mitch be enough to keep him safe?
Start the Big Bend Series with Love's Legacy

**Available at your favorite bookseller!!**

Join Blake's email list to get advance notice of new books and receive his occasional newsletter:

www.blakeallwood.com

<table>
<tr><td>

## MM Romance
## By Blake Allwood

**Transitions Series**
Aiden Inspired
Suzie Empowered (MF Romance)
Bobby Transformed

**Chance Series**
Love By Chance
Another Chance With Love
Taking A Chance For Love

**Romantic Series**
Romantic Renovations (1)
Romantic Rescue (2)
Romantic Recon (3)

**Melody Series**
Melody of the Heart
Melody of the Snow

**Road to Rocktoberfest Anthology**
Changing His Tune - 2022

**Coming Home Series (2023)**
A Long Way Home
Family Home
Discovering Home
Finding Home
Bound For Home
…and many more

**Novellas**
Tenacious
Moon's Place

</td><td>

## Romantic Fantasy
## By Adam J. Ridley

**Big Bend Series**
Love's Legacy (1)
Love's Heirloom (2)
Love's Bequest (3)

**The Witch Brothers Series**
Emerald Earth (1)
Diamond Air (2)
Ruby Fire (3)
Sapphire Water (4)

</td></tr>
</table>

Blake Allwood was born in west Tennessee, then moved to Kansas City MO after earning a degree in Early Childhood Education from Graceland College in Lamoni, Iowa. He met his husband Shaun in 1995 and they officially married in 2015, once gay marriage was legalized; although they still consider Valentines Day 1995 as their true "anniversary date". Twenty-two years later (2017), after fostering 12 children together, he and his husband sold their home, purchased an RV and began traveling the country with their two dogs.

Typically, Blake can be found relaxing in the RV or by the fire with his laptop and their Jack Russell Terrier, Buddy, curled up between his legs demanding attention. Denver, their Siberian Husky mix is often asleep at his feet or playing tug of war with Blake's husband.

Most of Blake's stories are inspired by the places they have visited in their ongoing travels. His first book, **_Aiden Inspired_**, was released in 2019 and he has now written over 20 books. In 2023 he is releasing the **_Coming Home_** series which is comprised of ten-plus sweet contemporary romance novels that are based on a fictional town in his home state of Tennessee.

Blake also writes under the pen name of Adam J. Ridley for his urban fantasy fans looking for stories revolving around gay characters. His first series is The Witch Brothers Saga, starting with **Emerald Earth**.

# BIBLIOPRIDE.COM

## BOOKS BY LGBTQ+ AUTHORS